MW00815295

NOIR
ISTHENEW
BLACK
DARBOE

F2 FAIRSQUARE
COMICS

NOIR IS THE NEW BLACK
Volume 1. Second Printing.
This title is a publication of FairSquare Comics, LLC.
608S Dunsmuir Ave #207, Los Angeles, CA 90036.

RIGHTS, MEDIA & LICENSING | fairsquarecomics@gmail.com +1(323) 405-9401
CEO & PUBLISHER | Fabrice Sapolsky

Cover illustration inspired by Shutterstock image 1376915186.
PRINTED IN THE USA by MIXAM.

SPECIAL THANKS
Kristal Adams, Ethan Sapolsky, Margot Atwell @KickStarter, Dillie Farris, Don Nguyen, Chris Allo, Mark Waid, Rickey Purdin, Francis Lombard, Julian Voloj, Karama Horne, Deron Bennett, Joseph Illidge.

DEDICATED TO BREONNA TAYLOR, GEORGE FLOYD, RAYSHARD BROOKS, DANIEL PRUDE, ATATIANA JEFFERSON, AURA ROSSER, STEPHON CLARK, BOTHAM JEAN, PHILANDO CASTILLE, ALTON STERLING, MICHELLE CUSSEAUX, FREDDY GRAY, JANISHA FONVILLE, ERIC GARNER, AKAI GURLEY, GABRIELLA NEVAREZ, TAMIR RICE, MICHAEL BROWN, TANISHA ANDERSON, TRAYFORD PELLERIN, DIJON KIZZEE, DAMIAN DANIELS, JONATHAN PRICE, WALTER WALLACE JR., SINCERE PIERCE, A.J. CROOMS, RODNEY APPLEWHITE, CASEY GOODSON JR., MAURICE GORDON, JOSHUA FEAST, ANDRE' HILL , DOLAL IDD, CARL DORSEY III, PATRICK WARREN SR., FREDERICK COX, XZAVIER HILL, KURT REINHOLD, MCHALE ROSE, MARVIN D. SCOTT III, DAUNTE WRIGHT, MATTHEW WILLIAMS, ANDREW BROWN, ASHTON PINKE and all the Black Americans who lost their lives because of Police brutality. You'll ALWAYS be remembered.

Be the change. Peace.

COMICS FOR THE REST OF US
WWW.FAIRSQUARECOMICS.COM

NOIR: noun *[nwär]*
Genre of crime fiction featuring hard-boiled cynical characters and bleak sleazy settings. Black Noir, brought to life by black American writers from the 1960s on, takes the Noir concept to the next level. Black Noir is past, present and future.

THE STATE OF AFFAIRS

LETTERING
ANDWORLD STUDIOS

COLLECTION CURATED AND EDITED BY
FABRICE SAPOLSKY WITH TC HARRIS

MARTINBROUGH

FOREWORD

BY SHAWN MARTINBROUGH

I'm always surprised when people ask me what does the word "Noir" mean?

I immediately check myself. Am I being elitist? Or an art house snob?
The term "Noir" has been part of my visual lexicon for decades. I see it everywhere. In film, television, music videos, books and graphic novels. Especially graphic novels.

As an aspiring artist and huge comic book fan, I gravitated to the Noir inspired works of artists Alex Toth, Frank Miller, Mike Mignola, David Mazzuchelli, Bill Sienkiewicz and countless others. In turn, I developed my own, high contrast and a heavy use of shadows approach which some referred to as "Noir" style.

Technically, the word "Noir "is French for Black but the term is really used to describe a distinct visual approach to storytelling. It's a mood. A vibe.
The editor of the NOIR IS THE NEW BLACK anthology is writer, editor and artist Fabrice Sapolsky.

Fabrice co-created the character Spider-Man Noir for Marvel who made his feature film debut in the Academy Award-winning animated film SPIDER-MAN: INTO THE SPIDER VERSE. Spider-Man Noir was the dapper dressed, black and white character (voiced by Nicolas Cage) who saved the world alongside Miles Morales.

Clearly, Fabrice is also a huge fan of Noir and has a deep love of comic books or as they're referred to in his native home of France, *Bande dessinées*.
When Fabrice first shared his vision of a showcase for new and lesser known writers and artists of color to tell their stories with me, I was proud and honored to lend my voice to write this foreword.

With NOIR IS THE NEW BLACK, Fabrice has used his editorial skills to assemble an eclectic group of creators and curate their voices into a compelling anthology. Spanning various historical time periods and even crossing into Afrofuturism, the featured stories are told in completely different styles but are all unified through the Noir esthetic.

NOIR IS THE NEW BLACK is a great achievement. Once this collection is released, absorbed and discussed, I am certain that more folks will know what the term "Noir" means.

Shawn Martinbrough is the author of How To Draw Noir Comics: The Art and Technique of Visual Storytelling and the artist of Batman: Detective Comics, Luke Cage Noir, Thief of Thieves and Prometheé 13 :13.

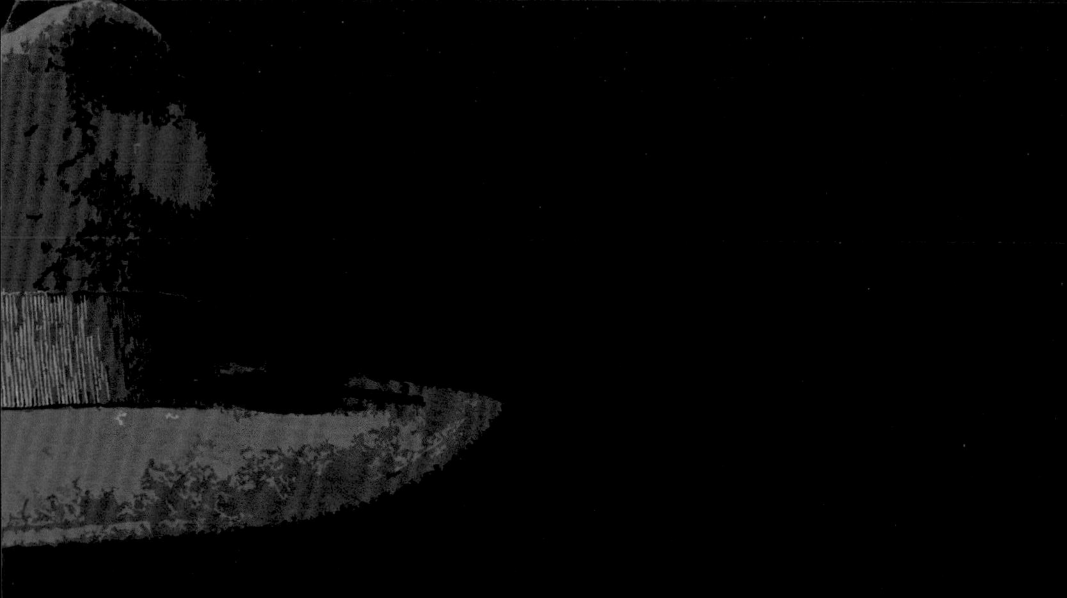

VERA'S LIST

STORY: TYRONE FINCH   ART: TODD HARRIS

COLORS: TOYIN AJETUNMOBI

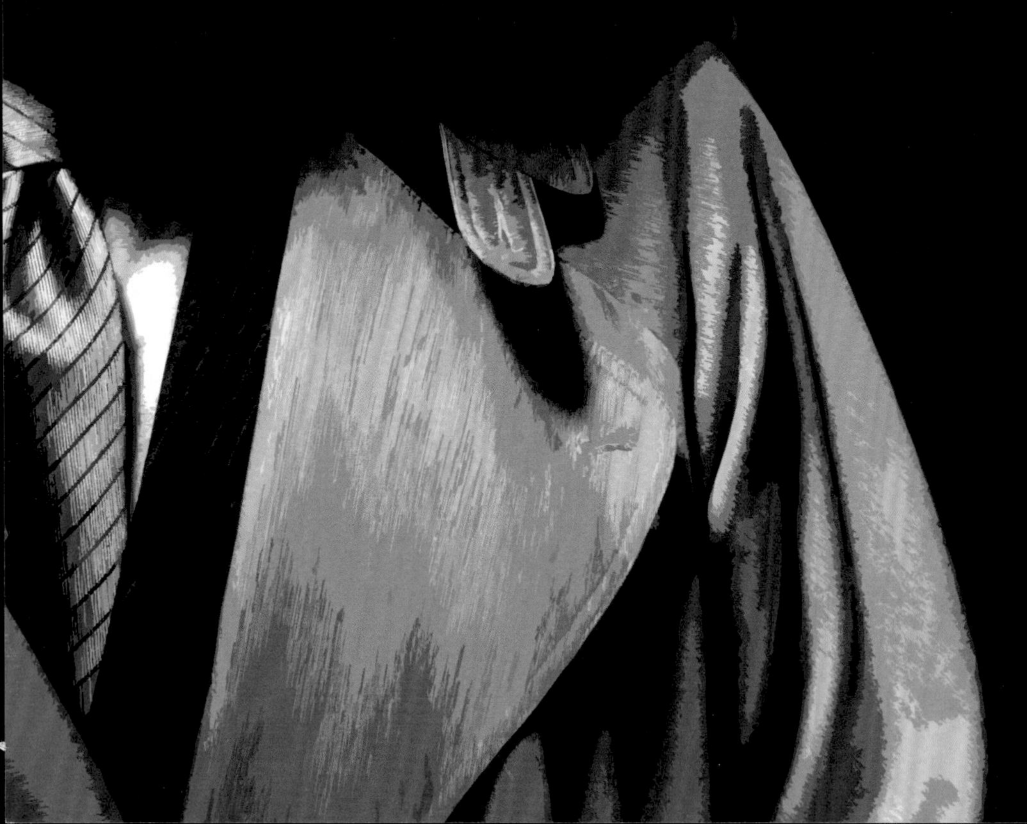

AURORA, ILLINOIS. 1946.
IT'S NOT JUST THE BROOM AND THE COVERALLS THAT MAKE ME INVISIBLE.

IT'S ALSO THE COLOR OF MY SKIN.

I'M JUST ANOTHER BLACK MAN WORKING ANOTHER DEAD END JOB.

EVEN TO PEOPLE WHO SHOULD KNOW BETTER.

BUT SHE'S SMART ENOUGH TO NOTICE WHAT HER HENCHMEN DON'T.

AND I'M MADE.

WOMEN...

OOOF!
WHEN YOU NEED THEM TO IGNORE YOU, THEY NEVER DO.

BUT BLAMING HER ISN'T FAIR.

IT'S MY OWN DAMNED FAULT.
THUMP

I'VE GOT A WEAKNESS FOR OVERPRICED ITALIAN SHOES... AND NOW THEY'RE SCUFFED.

I WAKE UP WITH A HEADACHE AND 12,000 FEET OF SKY BETWEEN ME AND THE GROUND.

WHY DOESN'T YOUR GUN HAVE ANY BULLETS IN IT?

BECAUSE I KNOW HOW IT FEELS TO KILL SOMEONE. AND I DON'T ENJOY IT.

NICE PIECE OF HARDWARE LIKE THIS SHOULD BE PUT TO USE. HOW MUCH WILL YOU TAKE FOR IT?
IT'S NOT FOR SALE. IT BELONGED TO MY BROTHER ERIC.

IS HE GOING TO COME LOOKING FOR IT?
ONLY IF HE CAN FIGURE A WAY TO DIG HIMSELF OUT FROM UNDER SIX FEET OF DIRT.

NATURAL CAUSES?
NOT UNLESS SHOTGUNS GROW ON TREES.

YOU'VE BEEN SHADOWING ME FOR TWO WEEKS. WHY?
THREE WEEKS. AND I WASN'T SHADOWING YOU. I WAS SHADOWING VERA.

AND WHO IS VERA?
THE WOMAN SITTING NEXT TO YOU.

SURPRISE.
YOU TOLD ME YOUR NAME WAS PEARL.

YOU TWO AN ITEM?
NOT A CHANCE. VERA ALSO BELONGED TO MY BROTHER.

YOU SEEM TO BE LOOKING AFTER A LOT OF HIS THINGS.
I PROMISED ERIC THAT I'D KEEP HER OUT OF TROUBLE.

THEN YOU'RE NOT GOOD AT KEEPING PROMISES.
VERA'S CRAZY. THAT MAKES IT HARDER.

SO WHAT'S YOUR PLAY?
NO PLAY. I'M GOING TO KILL YOU.

DO I GET TO KNOW WHY?
I MADE A LONG LIST OF THE PEOPLE RESPONSIBLE FOR ERIC'S DEATH. YOU'RE NUMBER SEVEN ON IT.

IF YOU KNOW WHO KILLED YOUR HUSBAND, YOU SHOULD TELL THE POLICE. I HAVE A FEW OFFICERS ON MY PAYROLL THAT ARE VERY GOOD LISTENERS.
THANK YOU, BUT I SPOKE TO THE POLICE. INVESTIGATING THE MURDER OF A BLACK CABBIE DIDN'T SEEM TO BE A PRIORITY FOR THEM.

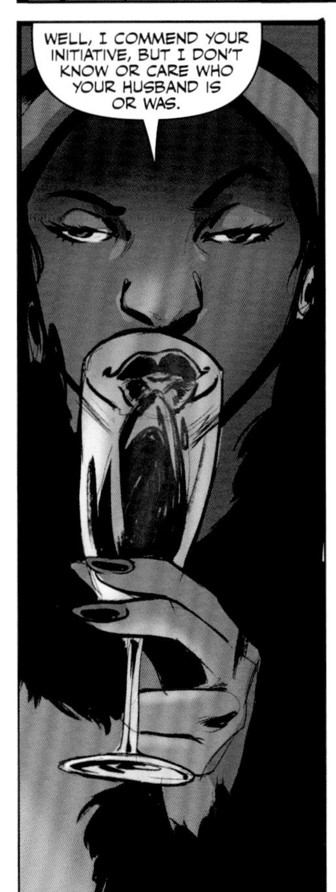
WELL, I COMMEND YOUR INITIATIVE, BUT I DON'T KNOW OR CARE WHO YOUR HUSBAND IS OR WAS.

NO, BUT YOU RUN COKE AND HEROIN FROM 110TH STREET TO GUN HILL.
AND YOU TITHE TWENTY PERCENT TO JOE WICKLUND IN THE BRONX. AND HE RUNS GUNS OUT OF PANAMA TO--
OHH, VERY INTERESTING.

TOLD YOU SHE'S CRAZY.
NOT CRAZY. BRILLIANT.
VERA UNDERSTANDS THE INTERCONNECTEDNESS OF ALL THINGS. AND SOMEHOW, I'M PART OF THE INTRICATE WEB THAT MURDERED HER HUSBAND.

Y'KNOW, LEVI IS ALSO ON MY LIST. BUT HE'S FAMILY SO HE GETS TO DIE LAST.
NO, VERA. LEVI IS GOING TO DIE IN ABOUT TWO MINUTES.

THAT LITTLE DERRINGER YOU'RE HOLDING PACKS ONLY ONE BULLET. AND AFTER YOU FIRE IT, MY BOYS ARE GOING TO KILL THE TWO OF YOU SO FAST THAT WE'LL ALL BE RIDING TO HELL ON THE EXACT SAME BOBSLED.

SO AGAIN I ASK YOU, WHAT'S YOUR PLAY?

BANG

LIKE I SAID, VERA'S CRAZY.
KRA-KOOOOM

I DON'T ENJOY KILLING.

I ALSO DON'T ENJOY COUGH SYRUP.

BUT WHEN MY THROAT IS DRY AND SCRATCHY...

I TAKE MY MEDICINE.
AAAHHHHHH!

I'D ALWAYS HOPED THAT I'D HAVE SOME HUGE EPIPHANY RIGHT BEFORE DYING. SOMETHING THAT WOULD EXPLAIN WHY MY LIFE BECAME SUCH A MESS .

BUT INSTEAD, ALL I CAN DO IS REMEMBER A JOKE THAT ERIC ONCE TOLD ME.

QUESTION: WHAT DO YOU CALL A BLACK GUY WHO CAN FLY A PLANE?

SCREEEEEEE

ANSWER: YOU CALL HIM A PILOT.
VROOOOM

The End.

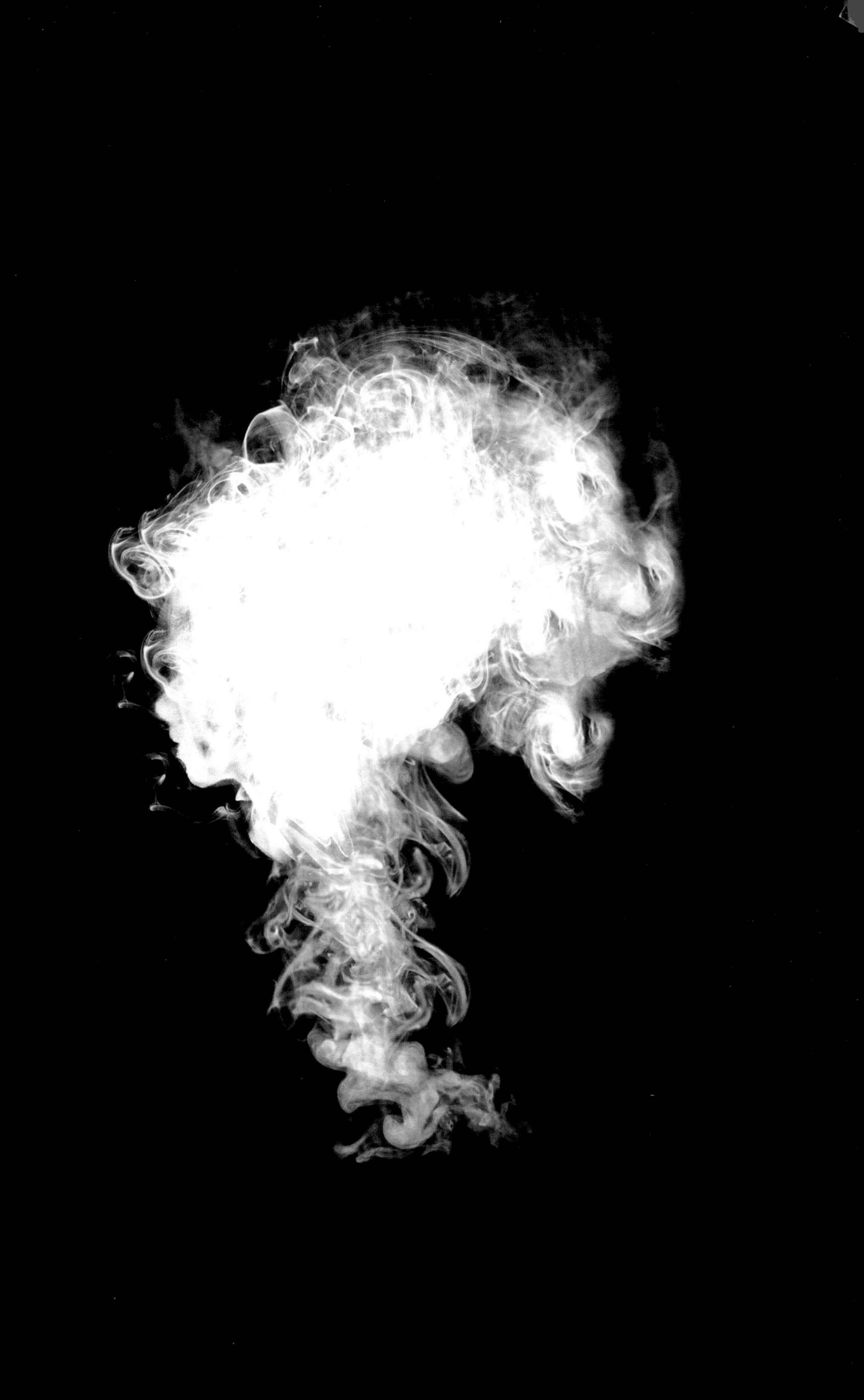

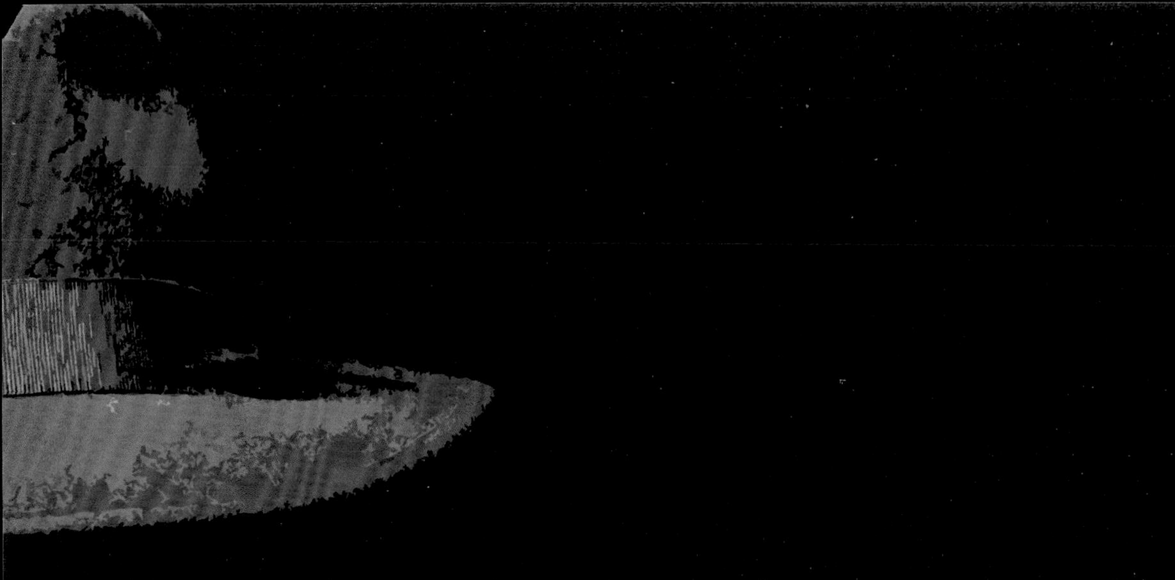

GEMINI VISIONS

STORY: BRANDON EASTON
ART & COLORS: DIETRICH SMITH

BALTIMORE, MARYLAND.
THIS PAST NOVEMBER.
THE CALL WENT OUT AT 10:42 PM ON THE POLICE SCANNER.
I WAS ON THE SCENE AT 11:01 PM. I HAD HIGH HOPES WE'D FINALLY FOUND HER.

BUT IT WASN'T MY SISTER ASHLEY. JUST ANOTHER SAD GIRL WHOSE LIFE HAD BEEN SNUFFED OUT BY BEING IN THE WRONG PLACE AT THE WRONG TIME.
A.K.A. BALTIMORE CITY.

THIS TOWN CAN BE SIMULTANEOUSLY MIRACULOUS AND HORRIFYING. BRIMMING WITH DIVINITY AND MORTAL SIN. A PERFECT CROSSROADS OF HUMAN POTENTIAL AND FALLIBILITY.
LORRAINE, YOU'RE LUCKY I FOUND YOU BEFORE MCCASKILL. HE'S LOOKING FOR A REASON...ANY REASON...TO PUT YOU IN THE PEN.
AND PERFECTLY CORRUPT.

"GEMINI." YOU LOST YOUR LORRAINE PRIVILEGES AFTER YOU LET THEM BOUNCE ME OFF THE FORCE.
SUCH A SELECTIVE MEMORY.
FOR THE SAKE OF SELF-PRESERVATION. AND YOU'RE NOT ALLOWED TO SMOKE WHEN ON DUTY. OR HAVE THE RULES CHANGED FOR YOUR BENEFIT?

HOW'D YOU GET HERE SO FAST? THE CALL JUST WENT OUT AND YOU'RE ASSIGNED TO NORTHEAST THESE DAYS.
IT AIN'T ASHLEY.

THEY GOT A NAME ALREADY? EITHER YOU'VE BECOME A HOLMESIAN GENIUS OR--
OR WHAT? YOU KNOW GODDAMN WELL THAT I'D HIT YOU UP FIRST IF WE FOUND A LEAD ON YOUR SISTER.
I PROTECTED YOU WHEN WE WERE PARTNERS AND I'M STILL PROTECTING YOUR UNGRATEFUL ASS NOW. THIS CITY TEARS THROUGH NAÏVE GIRLS LIKE TOILET PAPER AND--

WHHHHRRRR-WHOOP
604
POLICE
DAMMIT. THIS IS CAPTAIN MCCASKILL.

OFFICER MONTROSE, I HOPE TO GOD YOU'VE GOT A GOOD EXPLANATION WHY YOU'RE OUTSIDE OF YOUR BEAT AT AN ACTIVE CRIME SCENE SMOKING CIGARS WITH A DEPARTMENT WASHOUT?
ON SECOND THOUGHT, I DON'T WANT TO HEAR IT. GET OUTTA HERE NOW!
AND MS. JACKSON, IF I SEE YOU ANYWHERE NEAR ONE OF MY OFFICERS, I'LL HAVE YOU ARRESTED FOR INTERFERING WITH A POLICE INVESTIGATION.

AFRO AMERICAN
BEAUTY FOUND IN LAKE RULED ACCIDENTAL DEATH
"ACCIDENTAL DEATH?"
TO GET TO THE FOUNTAIN, SHE WOULD HAVE HAD TO SWIM THROUGH WATER COLD ENOUGH TO KILL HER AND THEN CLIMB THE LADDER BEFORE HYPOTHERMIA SET IN.
THERE ARE SMARTER AND FASTER WAYS TO COMMIT SUICIDE.
12! 12! 12!
HAPPY BIRTHDAY
ASH and LORRAINE THE GEMINI GIRLS
I NEED TO TALK TO LENNY. ASAP.
WHEN YOU NEEDED TO CATCH THE PULSE OF THE STREETS IN BALTIMORE, LEXINGTON MARKET WAS THE EPICENTER OF GOSSIP AND MALICE.
WORLD FAMOUS LEXINGTON MARKET SINCE 1782
AND THERE WAS ONE DUDE WHO KNEW IT ALL...
LENNY'S
LENNY SHOE-SHINE!
GEMINI JACKSON! MY EYES BEEN STARVING FOR A PRETTY FACE LATELY.
LEMME GUESS THE REASON YOU HERE...THAT GIRL THEY FOUND IN THE WATER, RIGHT?

THOSE POLICE BOYS BEEN PICKIN' GNAT SHIT OUTTA PEPPER TO RULE THAT AN ACCIDENTAL DEATH. I KNEW THAT GIRL...SHELLY WAS HER NAME, USED TO MESS AROUND WITH THE HUSTLERS OVER BY NORTH AND GREENMOUNT.
THE POLICE HAVE A VESTED INTEREST IN MISDIRECTION. YOU KNOW ANYTHING ELSE ABOUT HER?

NOT TOO MUCH, OTHER THAN THE FACT SHE WAS A PART-TIME WAITRESS AT THE BLUE PYRAMID CLUB. YOU MIGHT WANT TO ASK ABOUT THEM OTHER GIRLS THAT WENT MISSIN'.
OTHER GIRLS?
HEH, ALL I'M GONNA SAY IS THAT IF YOU PLANNIN' TO VISIT, TAKE CARE LITTLE LADY...
...SOME OF THE SHADIEST "YO'S" IN TOWN HANG OUT THERE AT NIGHT.

HEY GIRL, WELCOME TO THE BLUE PYRAMID. YOU HERE FOR THE INTERVIEW SESSION?
NO, I JUST GOT IN FROM PHILLY, LOOKING FOR MY OLD ROOMMATE SHELLY. IS SHE WORKING TONIGHT?

NO...SHELLY DON'T WORK HERE ANYMORE. SHE...
I'M LAQUITA, I WORKED WITH SHELLY A FEW TIMES. NICE GIRL, BUT SHE DIDN'T GET ALONG WITH OUR CLIENTELE.
CLIENTELE?

TEXT ME TONIGHT. CAN'T TALK NOW, BUT SHELLY DESERVES MORE THAN SHE GOT.
I'LL TELL THE BOSS YOU LOOKING FOR A GIG. CHECK BACK TOMORROW, HE'LL BE HERE WAITING TO MEET WITH THE NEW GIRLS.
EXIT
"CLIENTELE?" NEW GIRLS? IT DIDN'T TAKE A ROCKET SCIENTIST TO DEDUCE THAT THE BLUE PYRAMID WAS MORE THAN JUST A NIGHTCLUB FOR STREET THUGS.

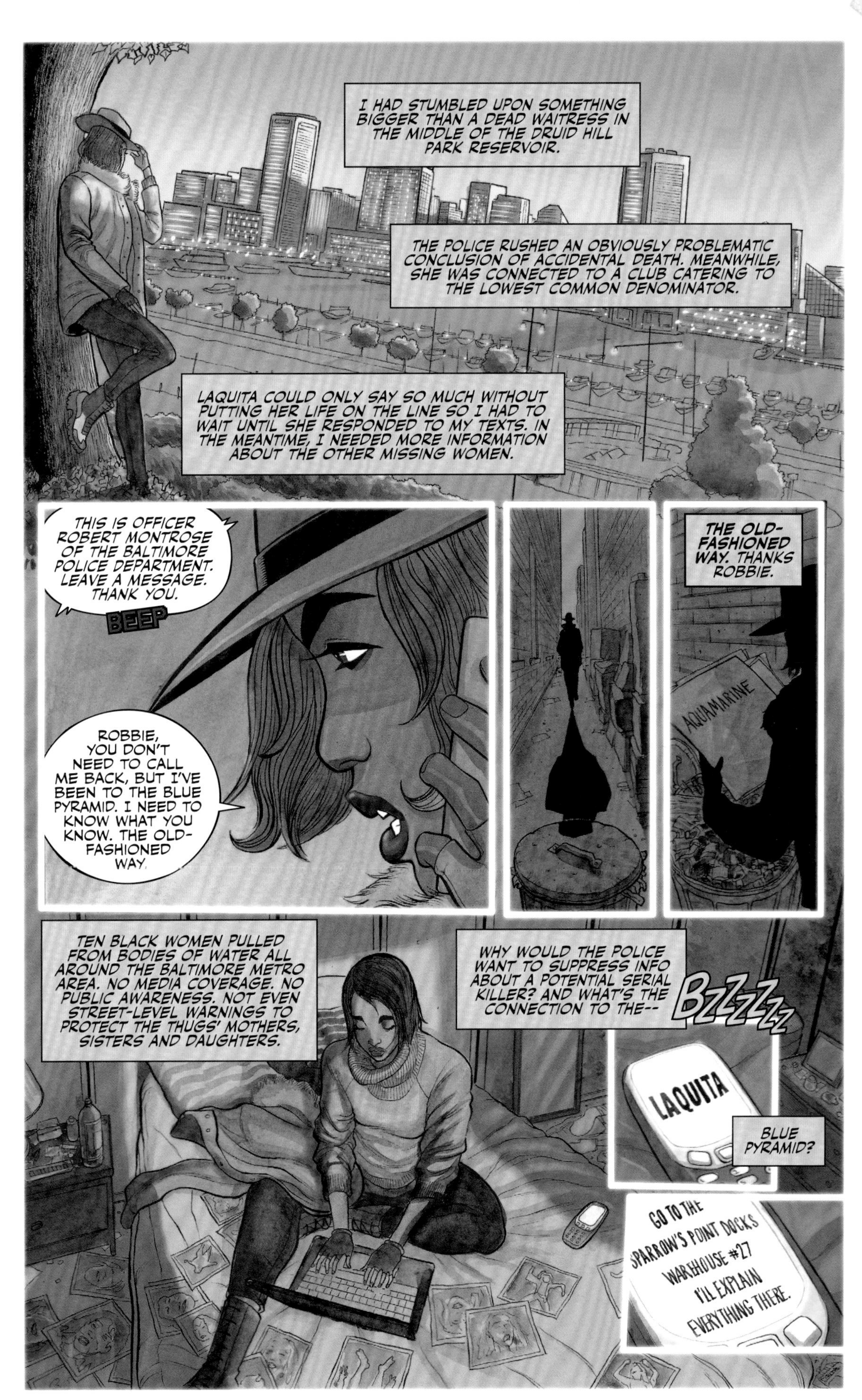
I HAD STUMBLED UPON SOMETHING BIGGER THAN A DEAD WAITRESS IN THE MIDDLE OF THE DRUID HILL PARK RESERVOIR.
THE POLICE RUSHED AN OBVIOUSLY PROBLEMATIC CONCLUSION OF ACCIDENTAL DEATH. MEANWHILE, SHE WAS CONNECTED TO A CLUB CATERING TO THE LOWEST COMMON DENOMINATOR.
LAQUITA COULD ONLY SAY SO MUCH WITHOUT PUTTING HER LIFE ON THE LINE SO I HAD TO WAIT UNTIL SHE RESPONDED TO MY TEXTS. IN THE MEANTIME, I NEEDED MORE INFORMATION ABOUT THE OTHER MISSING WOMEN.
THIS IS OFFICER ROBERT MONTROSE OF THE BALTIMORE POLICE DEPARTMENT. LEAVE A MESSAGE. THANK YOU.
BEEP
ROBBIE, YOU DON'T NEED TO CALL ME BACK, BUT I'VE BEEN TO THE BLUE PYRAMID. I NEED TO KNOW WHAT YOU KNOW. THE OLD-FASHIONED WAY.
THE OLD-FASHIONED WAY. THANKS ROBBIE.
AQUAMARINE
TEN BLACK WOMEN PULLED FROM BODIES OF WATER ALL AROUND THE BALTIMORE METRO AREA. NO MEDIA COVERAGE. NO PUBLIC AWARENESS. NOT EVEN STREET-LEVEL WARNINGS TO PROTECT THE THUGS' MOTHERS, SISTERS AND DAUGHTERS.
WHY WOULD THE POLICE WANT TO SUPPRESS INFO ABOUT A POTENTIAL SERIAL KILLER? AND WHAT'S THE CONNECTION TO THE--
BZZZZZ
LAQUITA
BLUE PYRAMID?
GO TO THE SPARROW'S POINT DOCKS WAREHOUSE #27 I'LL EXPLAIN EVERYTHING THERE.

27
SPARROW'S POINT. A RUST-BELT RELIC OF BALTIMORE'S BLUE-COLLAR GOLDEN AGE. NOW A CLAPTRAP OF OLD MILLS PACKED WITH BAD INTENTIONS.
LAQUITA MUST HAVE NEEDED EXTREME DISCRETION TO MEET ME HERE. BUT, I NEVER TRAVEL ALONE.

LAQUITA SENDS HER REGARDS!
WHA--?!

WHOK
UGG!

DUMB BITCH! YOU SHOULD HAVE BROUGHT PROTECTION!

BLAM
BLAM
I NEVER TRAVEL ALONE.

A PRIEST? THIS IS MUCH BIGGER THAN I IMAGINED. MUCH BIGGER.
BALTIMORE CAN BE MIRACULOUS AND HORRIFYING. DIVINE AND SINFUL.

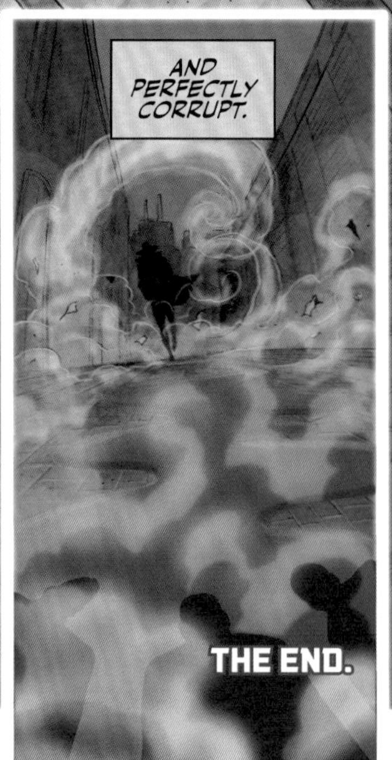
AND PERFECTLY CORRUPT.
THE END.

OUSLEY
STORY: GREG BURNHAM
ART: MARCUS WILLIAMS
COLORS: PARIS ALLEYNE
©Greg Burnham & Marcus Williams

**IT'S TRUE. THIS OCCURRED DURING PRESIDENT CLINTON'S TERM AS GOVERNOR OF ARKANSAS.*

OF ALL THE NIGHTS TO BE PULLED OVER FOR "DRIVING WHILE BLACK", HOW DID I GET SO LUCKY?
GLBMDW

CAN I HELP YOU OFFICER?
YOU CAN HELP BY CAUTIOUSLY REACHING FOR YOUR LICENSE AND REGISTRATION... OH SHIT!!!
LT. OUSLEY?! WHY THE HELL ARE YOU DRIVING SO SLOW?

JUST OUT HERE TRYING TO "LOOK NATURAL" WHILE GATHERING INTEL FROM MY INFORMANT BACK THERE.

MMMMMMM HMMMMM!

I'D LIKE TO GATHER SOME INTEL FROM THAT PHILLY MYSELF, IF YOU KNOW WHAT I MEAN.

I'M SIXTEEN YOU FREAKIN' CREEP!!

ALRIGHT GIL, YOU'VE WASTED ENOUGH OF MY TIME TONIGHT.
I GOTTA GET THIS KID HOME BEFORE HER PARENTS PUT OUT AN APB.
YESSIR. BUT DO ME A FAVOR...

STOP DRIVING LIKE YOU HAVE BODIES IN THE TRUNK. YOU ALREADY FIT THE DESCRIPTION.
NO MATTER HOW HIGH YOU RANK, YOU'RE ALWAYS GONNA FIT THE DESCRIPTION OUT HERE.

COULDN'T EVEN CUSS HIM OUT FOR THAT NONSENSE. LIFE'S FUNNY THAT WAY. RIGHT NOW MY ENTIRE CAREER IS ON THE LINE, WHEN JUST AN HOUR EARLIER, I WAS RIDING OUT MY UNEVENTFUL SHIFT, IN DREAMLAND OF ALL PLACES. AND THEN...THE PHONE RANG.
9:30 PM
OUSLEY... I UHH, I'M KINDA IN A TOUGH SPOT.
AND YOU KNOW...YOU ALWAYS SAY I SHOULD CALL YOU IF I'M IN TROUBLE SO...
WHERE ARE YOU?
I'VE LEARNED TO IGNORE THE KID'S CONSPIRACY RAMBLINGS. LET HER TELL IT, THE UNITED STATES GOVERNMENT HAS BEEN IN CAHOOTS WITH SOUTH AMERICAN DRUG DEALERS FOR OVER A DECADE.
YEP...OUR OWN GOVERNMENT IS RESPONSIBLE FOR THE DRUG AND GUN PROBLEMS THAT HAVE DECIMATED OUR COMMUNITIES. SOUNDS RIDICULOUS...DOESN'T IT?

AND THEN YOU WITNESS FIRST HAND...A GROUP OF THUGS DUMPING A CRATE OF GUNS IN A RANDOM ALLEY.
AK-47
OK, HOLD ON, I'M GONNA NEED YOU TO SLOW DOWN BIG FELLA.
NOW THAT...WAS A BAD MOVE!
CRACK
SO I GUESS WE WON'T BE RESOLVING THIS AMICABLY, HUH?
PRETTY SURE THIS IS ABOVE YOUR PAY GRADE. LAST CHANCE TO WALK AWAY.

YEAH, NOT GONNA DO THAT.
SNAP
ALRIGHT, ENOUGH!
YOU HAVE NO IDEA WHAT YOU'RE DOING MAN!
YOU SHOULDA LET IT GO!
EASY.
OHHH, I'M GONNA LET SOMETHING GO ALRIGHT!
YOU MESSED WITH THE WRONG CREW TONIGHT BUDDY!
POW
SAY GOODBYE TO THE BAD GIRL!
OOOOPS.
DAMN THAT SHOT WAS TERRIBLE.
CRUNCH

AND THAT LEADS ME HERE. DIGGING A DITCH AT 1:00AM IN THE MIDDLE OF NOWHERE.

NORMALLY I'D JUST CALL THIS IN TO THE PRECINCT, WRITE IT UP AND BE DONE. BUT THIS WAS NO ORDINARY EVENT.

APPARENTLY TIA WAS RIGHT. OUR GOVERNMENT IS CONSPIRING WITH SOUTH AMERICAN DRUG CARTELS, INJECTING DRUGS AND GUNS INTO OUR COMMUNITIES.
C.I.A. OFFICERS EH? SO WHERE DO WE GO FROM HERE BIG BROTHER?
NOT EXACTLY SURE, BUT IT LOOKS LIKE I HAVE SOME CLEANING UP TO DO.
CIA
U S
SPECIAL AGENT
ALSO, GOTTA WORK ON YOUR SHOOTING.
AND YOUR CATCH PHRASE.
YOU CAN'T JUST YELL OUT RANDOM MOVIE QUOTES BEFORE YOU SHOOT. ESPECIALLY WHEN THEY AREN'T APPLICABLE...
THE END?

THE BLACK CONSTABLE

STORY: NICK ALLEN   ART: MERVYN MCKOY

COLORS: JACKSON GODWIN

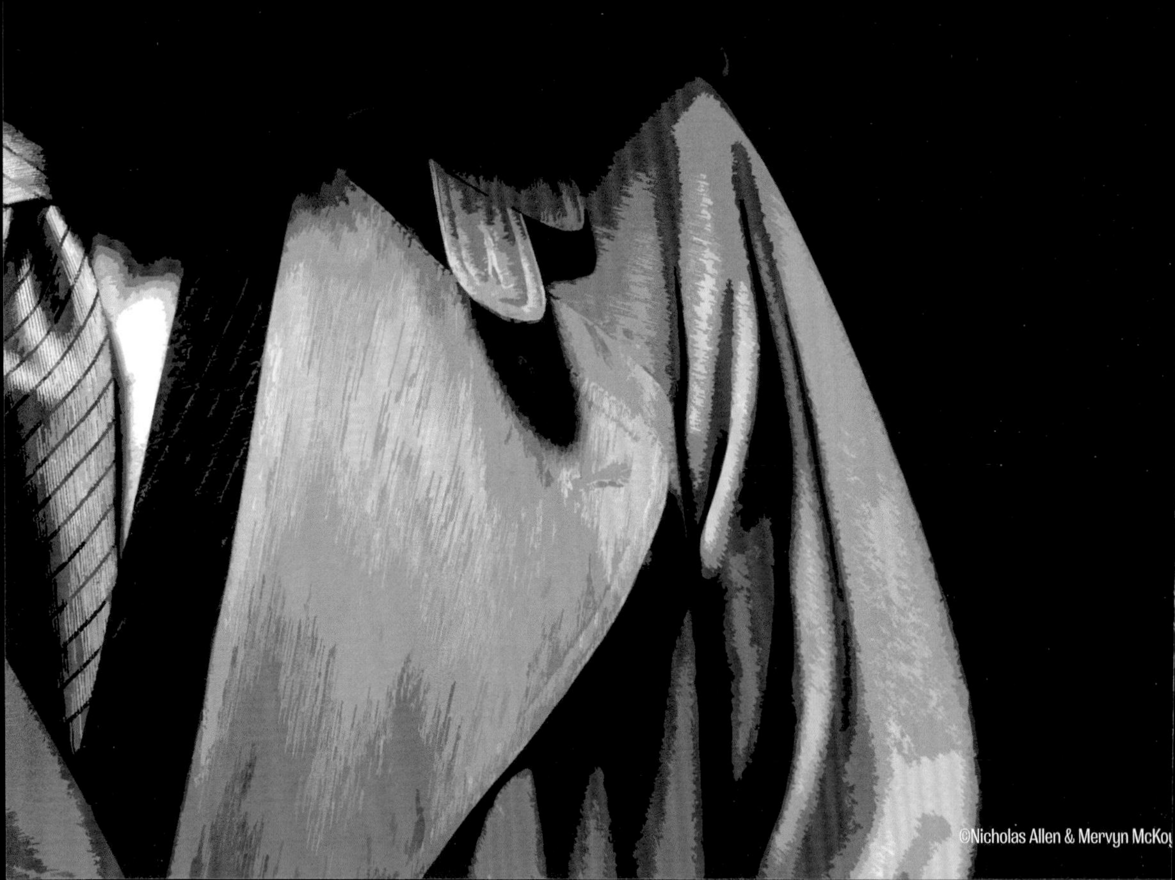

THE COLONY OF JAMAICA
FREEDOM.
IT WAS ALL I EVER YEARNED FOR.
TROT TROT TROT
BUT, WHAT IS FREEDOM WITHOUT A FUTURE?
HOW I WISH TO BE RID OF THIS FAUSTIAN BARGAIN I MAKE TIME AND TIME AGAIN...
EACH TRIAL, A THOUSAND ERRORS ALL TO CREATE ONE PERFECT ACT.
AS I ENTER, I CAN SENSE THEIR ENVY, THEIR LOATHING.
SIR.
BLOOD BOILS LIKE KETTLED WATER. I SHOULD NOT EXIST, I CAN NOT EXIST.
YET I DO. I AM A MAN LIKE NO OTHER. I AM EXCEPTIONAL, AND THEY HATE ME FOR IT.
MY, WHAT AN EXQUISITE BROOCH.
QUITE THE APPURTENANCE, YES? A FAMILY HEIRLOOM FROM HIS LATE FATHER, OR WAS IT YOUR MOTHER?
THE LORD. CHARLES ALLERDYCE, SUGAR MAGNATE AND MASTER OF THE BLACKBYRNE ESTATE AND ALL IT SURVEYS.
HIS RECENT FAILED AUCTION IS THE CAUSE OF THIS GATHERING. HE SUSPECTS NEGRO MEDDLING.
THE LIAISON. JAMES MORGAN, THE EAR OF JAMAICA'S GOVERNOR.
OUR GUEST, WHO MAY ASSIST IN RECRUITING A LARGER MILITARY DETACHMENT FOR CHARLES ALLERDYCE'S MACHINATIONS, PENDING MY REPORT.
GENTLEMEN, I REQUEST A CALL TO ORDER FOR THE RECITATION OF THE CONSTABLE'S FINAL REPORT.
AND MYSELF.
THE CONSTABLE.
I'VE BEEN CALLED IN FOR THE NIGHT'S ENTERTAINMENT, WHAT WILL MOST LIKELY BE A SUMMARY EXECUTION. I'M HERE BECAUSE OF...

NANNY.
THE INFAMOUS LEADER OF THE WINDWARD MAROONS.
AND THE ALLEGED MASTERMIND OF ALLERDYCE'S RECENT MISFORTUNE.
I GLEANED MUCH, DURING MY QUERIES.

THEY SAY THE POWERS SHE POSSESSES ARE NOT OF THIS WORLD.
SHE WIELDS A BLACKENED BLADE WHICH DRINKS THE BLOOD OF HER ENEMIES...
...AND HANDILY DISPATCHES SOLDIERS WITH THEIR OWN PELLET FIRE.

HER DEFEAT IS IMPOSSIBLE BECAUSE OF CLAIRVOYANT ENDOWMENTS.
APOCRYPHAL TALES. HER WAR...
...IS ONE OF INFORMATION, BOLSTERED BY THE GUILEFUL MAROON METHODOLOGY.

MAROONS, AS YOU KNOW, ARE THE UNTAMED VESTIGES OF OUR NATION'S PRIOR CONFLICT WITH THE SPANIARDS.
NOTHING MORE THAN SLAVES WITH TOO LONG A LEASH.
THE EVIDENCE AFFIRMS SHE HAD THE HELP OF MORE THAN...
...MERE SLAVES.

THE CHAPERON.
NEVILLE NEWCASTLE, MY NINTH 'ATTENDANT', HIS PREDECESSORS DIED UNDER "MYSTERIOUS" CIRCUMSTANCES. PEREMPTORILY EXILED TO THIS TASK AS PENANCE FOR DEBTS OWED TO THE BLACKBYRNE ESTATE.
HE EXISTS TO LEGITIMIZE MY INVESTIGATIONS AMONGST MY 'BETTERS'.
THE TEMERITY!

THE SOLICITOR.
HOW DARE YOU SLANDER THE NAME OF ONE OF OUR TRUSTED CIRCLE? WHY WASN'T THIS IN MY PRE-ACTION REPORT? BEST WE SEND HIM TO THE GALLOWS AND BE DONE WITH THIS!
SIR PATRICK HUGHENDEN II, ESQUIRE. SPECIAL COUNCIL TO THE BLACKBYRNE ESTATE IN EXTRA LEGAL AFFAIRS.
NEVILLE, HOLD ON A MOMENT. THIS SKIT AMUSES ME, AND I DO BELIEVE WE WILL PARTAKE IN SOME PERNICIOUS PAGEANTRY BY THE END OF IT. CONTINUE, BOY.

HOWEVER, UPON FURTHER INSPECTION, I DISCOVERED MY INITIAL SUPPOSITIONS MAY HAVE BEEN IN ERR.
I UNCOVERED THE INFORMANT'S IDENTITY ON THE EDGE OF THE BLACKBYRNE ESTATE.

MANY THANKS TO THE ASSISTANCE OF ONE OF LORD ALLERDYCE'S DRIVERS AND HIS CAT O' NINE.

AND THE INFLUENCE OF A GENEROUS BOON FROM A PAST CASE.
SO WAS A SOLUTION EXHUMED.

T'WAS ONE OF THE ESTATE'S OWN. A SLAVE ONCE HELD IN HIGH REGARD,
HYACINTH BECKFORD.

BAH HAH HAR
HAH HAH

WHAT, PRAY TELL, IS SO AMUSING?

...THAT YOUR ACCUSED IS DEAD! AS I WILL BE SOON FROM LAUGHTER. HYACINTH HAS BEEN RESTING BENEATH PORTLAND PARISH FOR OVER A YEAR NOW.

IT SEEMS YOU'LL BE JOINING HYACINTH, BOY! YOUR REPUTATION WAS QUITE THE FABLE. ALL THE BETTER, AND A FITTING END TO BEING A NEGRO'S NURSEMAID.
THIS NEEDS TO BE SETTLED POSTHASTE, ALL PATHS LEAD TO...

DEATH.
YOU'VE MADE A THOUSAND ERRORS, BOY. YOU KNOW THE RULE. FAILURE IS ALWAYS DEATH! WHY MUST WE FACILITATE THIS FARCE ANY LONGER?
I WOULD SAY WE ARE CERTAINLY OVERDUE FOR A GOOD HANGING, NEVILLE.
I'VE NO TIME TO SPARE.
A THOUSAND ERRORS...
YOUR BELL HAS ASSUREDLY TOLLED.
BAH HAH HAR
HAH HAH

BOOOOOM
BONG

CHUFF

BOOOM

BONG
THUK

BOOOOM

A THOUSAND ERRORS CONSEQUENTLY LEAD TO PAYING MS. HYACINTH BECKFORD A VISIT.
I FOUND HER RESTING PEACEFULLY... AMONG OTHER THINGS.

WHAT FOOL DEPREDATES THEIR OWN MOTHER'S MEMORY?
ONE WITH THE PRIVILEGE TO DO AS SUCH.

THEN YOU CONFESS TO USING ME AS A SCAPEGOAT, SOLICITOR?
I CONFESS TO NOTHING.

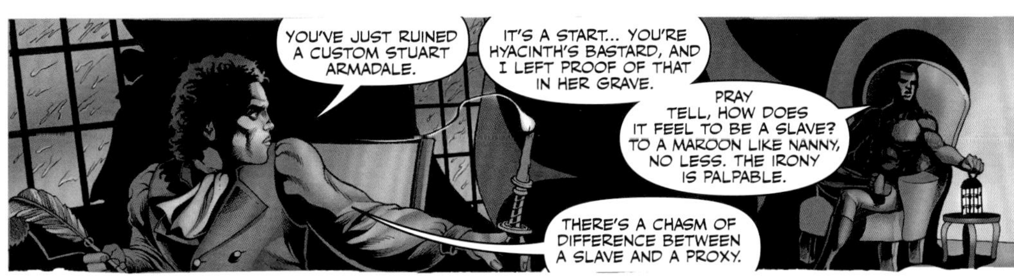
YOU'VE JUST RUINED A CUSTOM STUART ARMADALE.
IT'S A START... YOU'RE HYACINTH'S BASTARD, AND I LEFT PROOF OF THAT IN HER GRAVE.
PRAY TELL, HOW DOES IT FEEL TO BE A SLAVE? TO A MAROON LIKE NANNY, NO LESS. THE IRONY IS PALPABLE.
THERE'S A CHASM OF DIFFERENCE BETWEEN A SLAVE AND A PROXY.

YOUR CAREER IN LAW MAKES SENSE NOW. WHAT BETTER WAY TO HIDE THE TRUTH.
MY CAREER IN LAW ALLOWS ME TO UPHOLD JUSTICE.
WELL, I HOPE IT'S TAUGHT YOU HOW TO JUSTIFY MY "DEATH." I'LL BE MAKING A SWIFT DEPARTURE AS REWARD FOR NOT SHARING YOUR TRUTH.
THEY ALLOW YOU TO STAND IN THE ROOM WITH THE SEAT OF POWER. ISN'T IT INTOXICATING? YOU FEEL SPECIAL AND ON OCCASION YOU EVEN FEEL AS THOUGH YOU BELONG...
BUT ALL YOU ARE IS A MONGREL WHO PERFORMS A PARTICULAR TRICK THEY LIKE. SO, NO. YOU WON'T BE GOING ANYWHERE.
NANNY HAS PLANS FOR YOU.

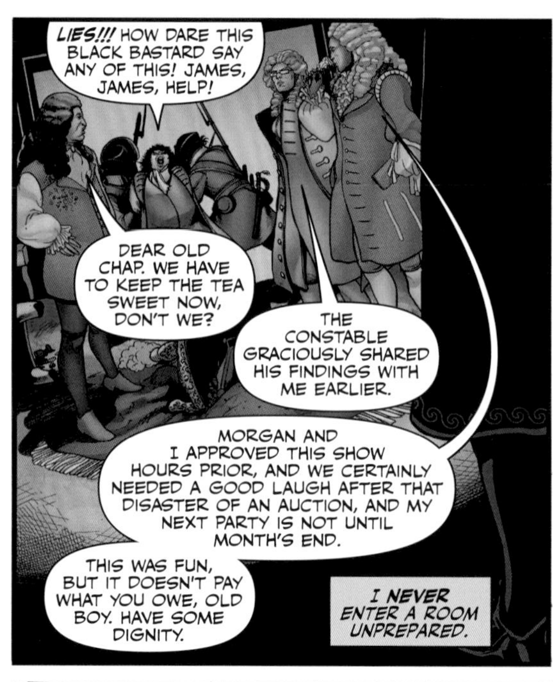

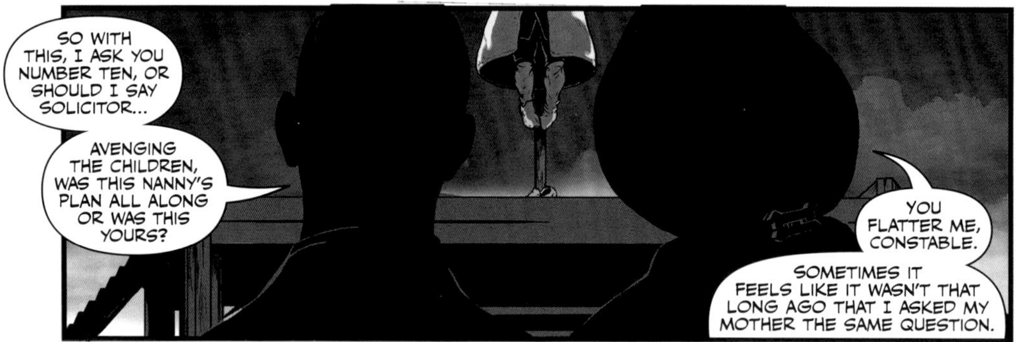

"TO WHICH SHE ALWAYS REPLIED: WHO AM I TO KNOW THE MIND OF A QUEEN?"

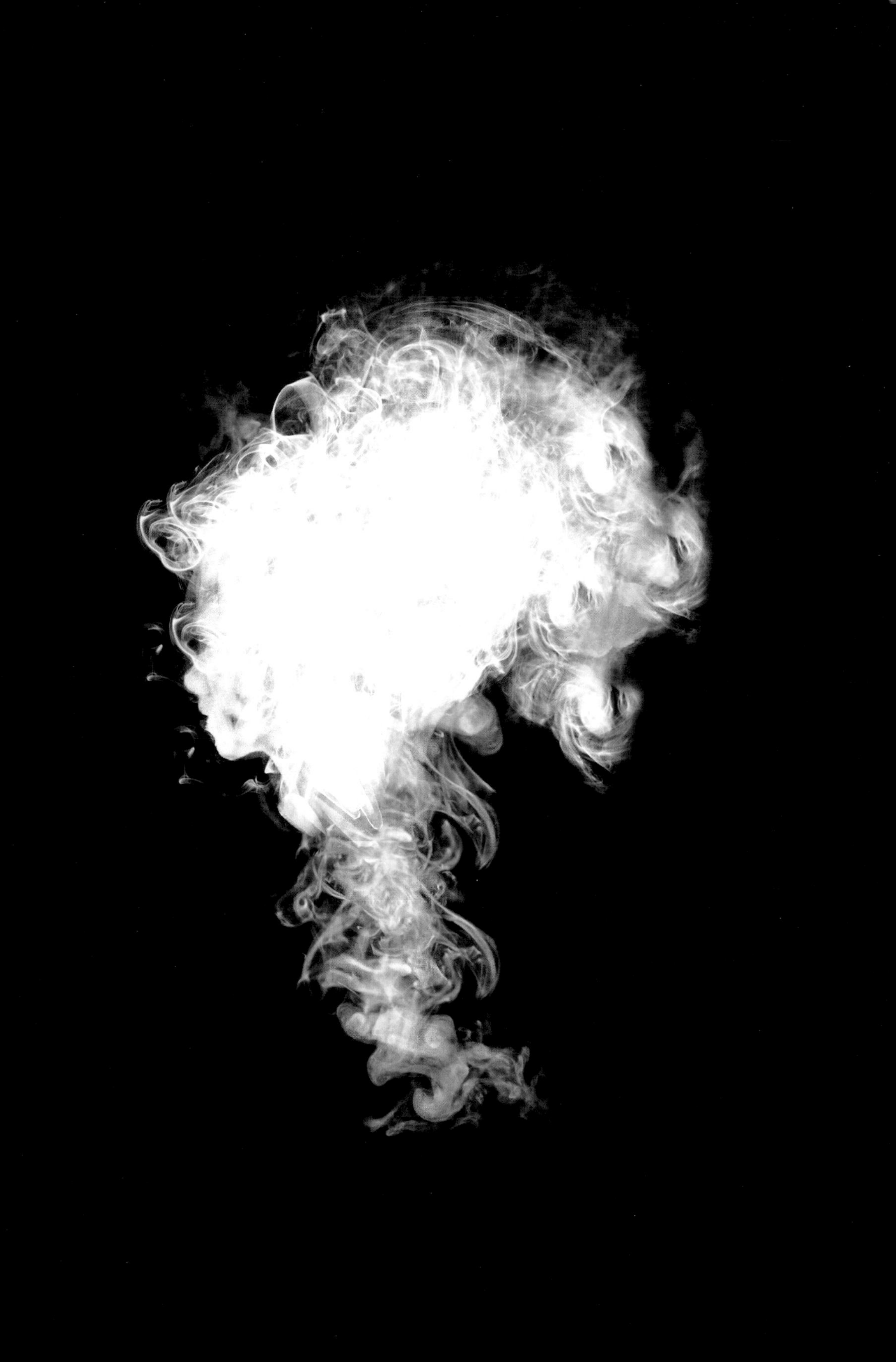

SOUTHERN HOSPITALITY

STORY: MIKHAIL HARDY ART: ELI JOHNSON

COLORS: ROBIN L.DAVIS

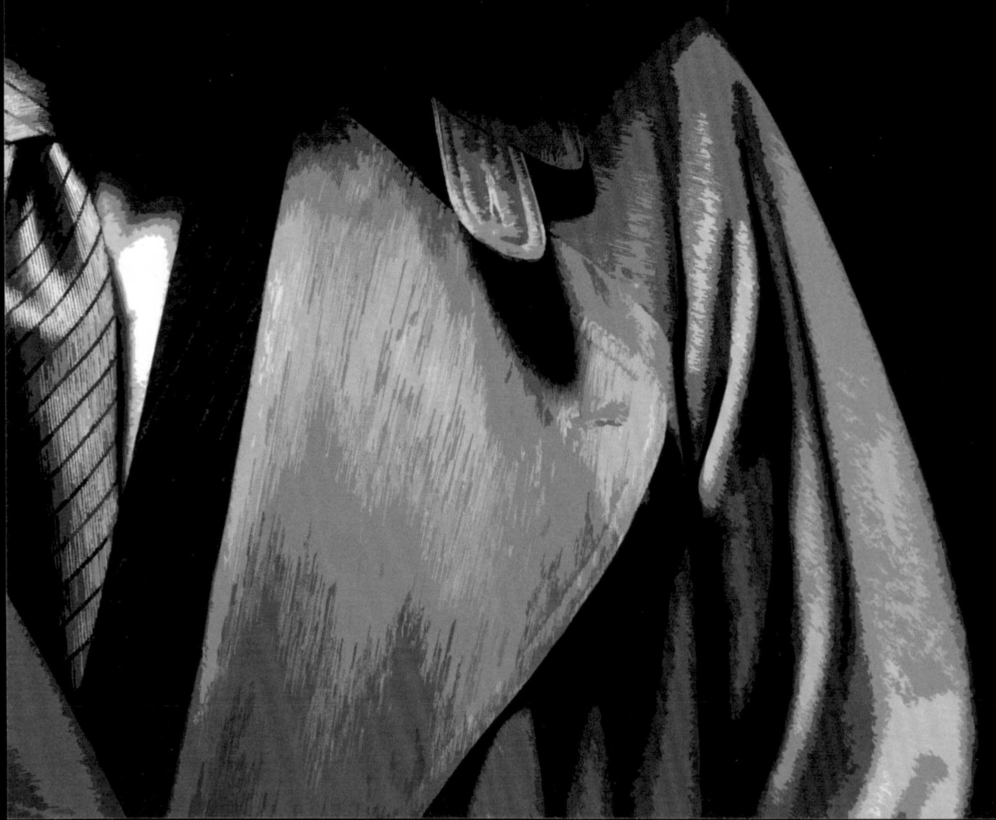

NO ONE CALLS ME JOHN JACKSON.
I GO BY J.J. EASY TO MEMORIZE, ESPECIALLY IN MY LINE OF WORK.

I WAS BORN AND RAISED HERE IN ALABAMA. BALDWIN COUNTY TO BE EXACT.

I'VE GIVEN THIS STATE MY LOVE, THIS COUNTRY MY HEART AND SOUL. BUT TODAY...
CRASH

IT'S TAKEN TOO MUCH...

... AND I THINK IT'S TIME TO GO HOME.

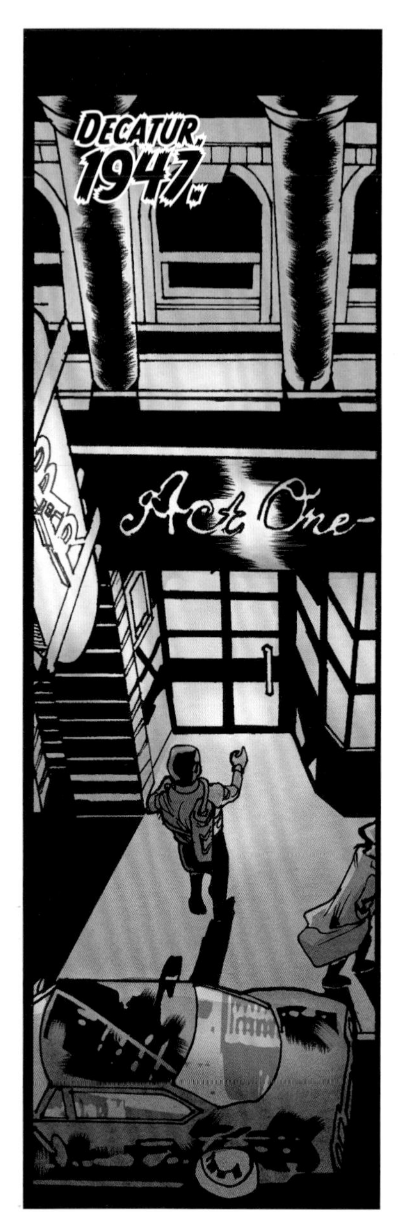
DECATUR, 1947.
Act One

HEY, IT'S MARK. YOU MIGHT WANT TO COME OVER HERE...

"...I THINK SOME TROUBLE JUST CAME IN."
EVENIN' GENTS.

I'LL HAVE A WHISKEY SHOT.
I THINK YOU'RE LOST, BOY!
I JUST WANNA SHARE A STORY WITH YOU GUYS AND I'LL BE ON MY WAY.

YOU'VE EITHER GOT A LOT OF BRASS OR YOU'RE REALLY DUMB. EITHER WAY, YOU'RE NOT LEAVING OUT THE SAME WAY YOU CAME IN.
FAIR ENOUGH. I'LL KEEP THIS SHORT.

WE THOUGHT JOINING YOUR RANKS WOULD EARN US SOME ACKNOWLEDGEMENT.

"WE THOUGHT FIGHTING YOUR WAR WOULD EARN US SOME RESPECT.

"YOU GAVE US OUR WORST AND WE TOOK IT ALL WITH A SMILE.

"MY FRIEND MARCUS, HE NEVER STOPPED SMILING.

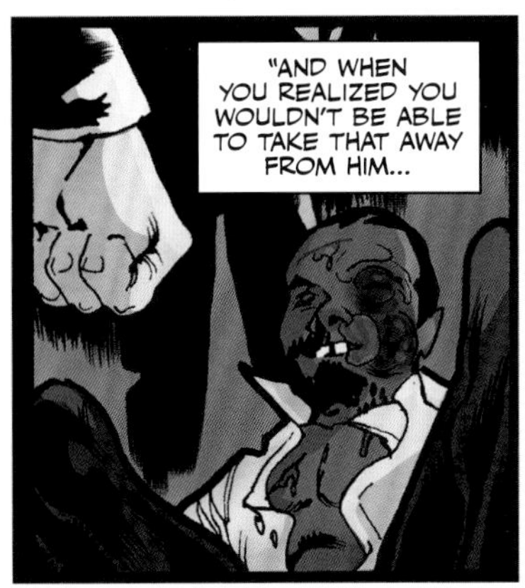
"AND WHEN YOU REALIZED YOU WOULDN'T BE ABLE TO TAKE THAT AWAY FROM HIM...

"...YOU TOOK AWAY THE MOST PRECIOUS THING FROM HIM."

"YOU TOOK AWAY HIS DREAM.

"YOU MURDERED MY FRIEND.
WELCOME HOME NIGGER!

ISN'T THAT RIGHT CAPTAIN SANDERS?

THIS HAS BEEN A LONG TIME COMING, HASN'T IT?

OKAY BOY! YOU'RE DONE!

PLUFFF
BLAM

WERE YOUR FRIENDS RAISED IN A BARN, SANDERS?

SON OF A...

BLAM

WOOOOO!
CREEESH
BLAMM BLAMM
YOU'RE DEAD YOU FUCKING MONKEY!
PRACK
CRASH

BLAMM
BLAM
BLAM
CRASH
KRIESH

TICK
TICK

HOLY SHI...

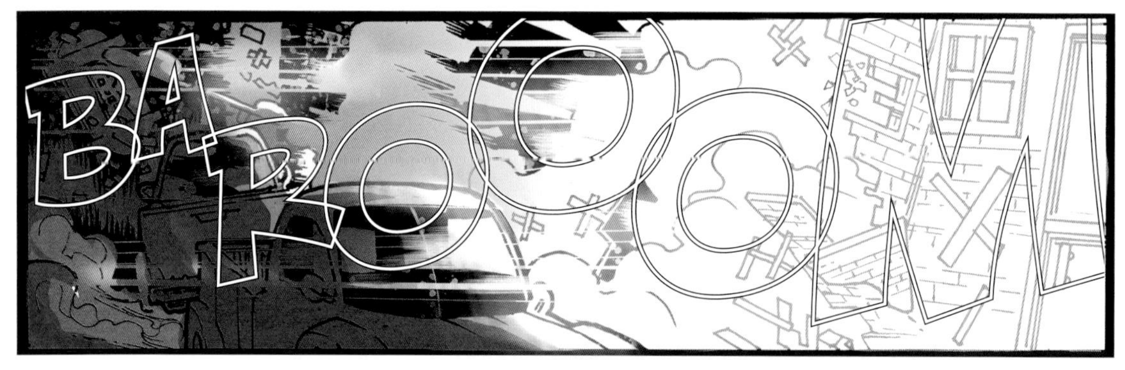
BAROOOOOM

THIS MOMENT ISN'T RAGE.

THIS IS RESILIENCE.

"MARCUS' DREAM WILL LIVE ON WITH ME."
BLAM

END.

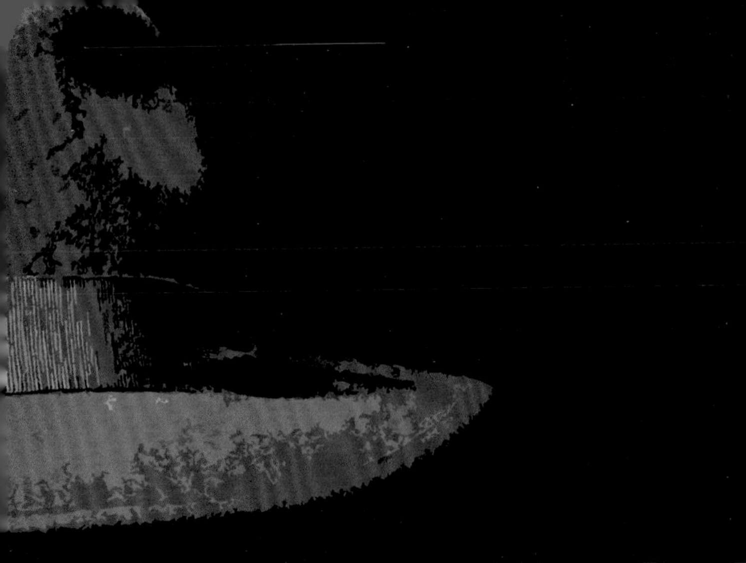

THE MESSAGE: JOSEPHINE SPEAKS

STORY: ROXXY HAZE
ART & COLORS: PAT MASIONI

Paris, France. Théâtre des Champs-Elysées. 1963.
MESDAMES ET MESSIEURS, PLEASE GIVE IT UP FOR MISS JOSEPHINE BAKER!
GREAT SHOW, JOSEPHINE, AS ALWAYS. SOMEONE DROPPED A LETTER FOR YOU. I PUT IT ON YOUR DESK.
MERCI, ÉMILIE.
OH NO!
BAKER
FRÉDÉRIC! PLEASE, HELP!
THE DEVIL

PEUT-ÊTRE... MAYBE...MAYBE YOU SHOULD POSTPONE YOUR TRIP. QUELQUES JOURS TOUT AU PLUS ?
S'IL VOUS PLAÎT, JOSÉPHINE! THIS WAS A DIRECT THREAT! DON'T YOU UNDERSTAND?
MMMM...
THIS ISN'T THE FIRST TIME SOMEONE HAS THREATENED YOU.
WE CAN'T CONTINUE TO TAKE THESE THREATS LIGHTLY. LET'S GO TO THE POLICE.
YOU MAY GO TO THE POLICE. BUT, I WILL NOT BE INTIMIDATED BY ANYONE.
PLEASE, DON'T GO! S'IL VOUS PLAÎT.
CHER FRÉDÉRIC, I HAVE TO. I GAVE MY WORD.
THEY'RE MY PEOPLE TOO.

Washington, D.C. a few days later.
THANK YOU, JEAN-BAPTISTE.
WE SHOULD BE THERE IN ABOUT 20 MIN. MISS BAKER.
WE'RE BEING FOLLOWED...
"IT'S A TRAP! HANG ON!..."
BANG

KOFFI, ARE YOU OKAY?
YES, MOTHER.
LET'S GET OUT OF HERE, HONEY.
HE'S STILL FOLLOWING US, MOM.
EVERYTHING'S GONNA BE ALRIGHT, BABY. CLOSE YOUR EYES.

WHAT DO YOU WANT!?
I KNOW YOU GOT OUR MESSAGE. YOU SHOULDN'T HAVE COME. WE DON'T WANT YOU HERE.
BUT... THIS IS MY HOME TOO. YOU **ARE** MY PEOPLE!
YOU SIT IN YOUR CASTLE, AND SING AND DANCE FOR THOSE CRACKERS IN EUROPE. AND YOU THINK YOU CAN SPEAK FOR US?
YOU ARE **THE DEVIL.**
NO, SHE'S NOT...
SHE'S MY MOTHER.
BANG
JEAN-BAPTISTE!
POLICE WILL BE HERE SOON MRS. BAKER. WE STILL CAN MAKE IT ON TIME FOR...

"...DR. KING'S FREEDOM MARCH."
I HAVE WALKED INTO THE PALACES OF KINGS AND QUEENS AND INTO THE HOUSES OF PRESIDENTS...
...AND MUCH MORE. BUT I COULD NOT WALK INTO A HOTEL IN AMERICA AND GET A CUP OF COFFEE. THAT IS WHY *I* ***SPEAK.***

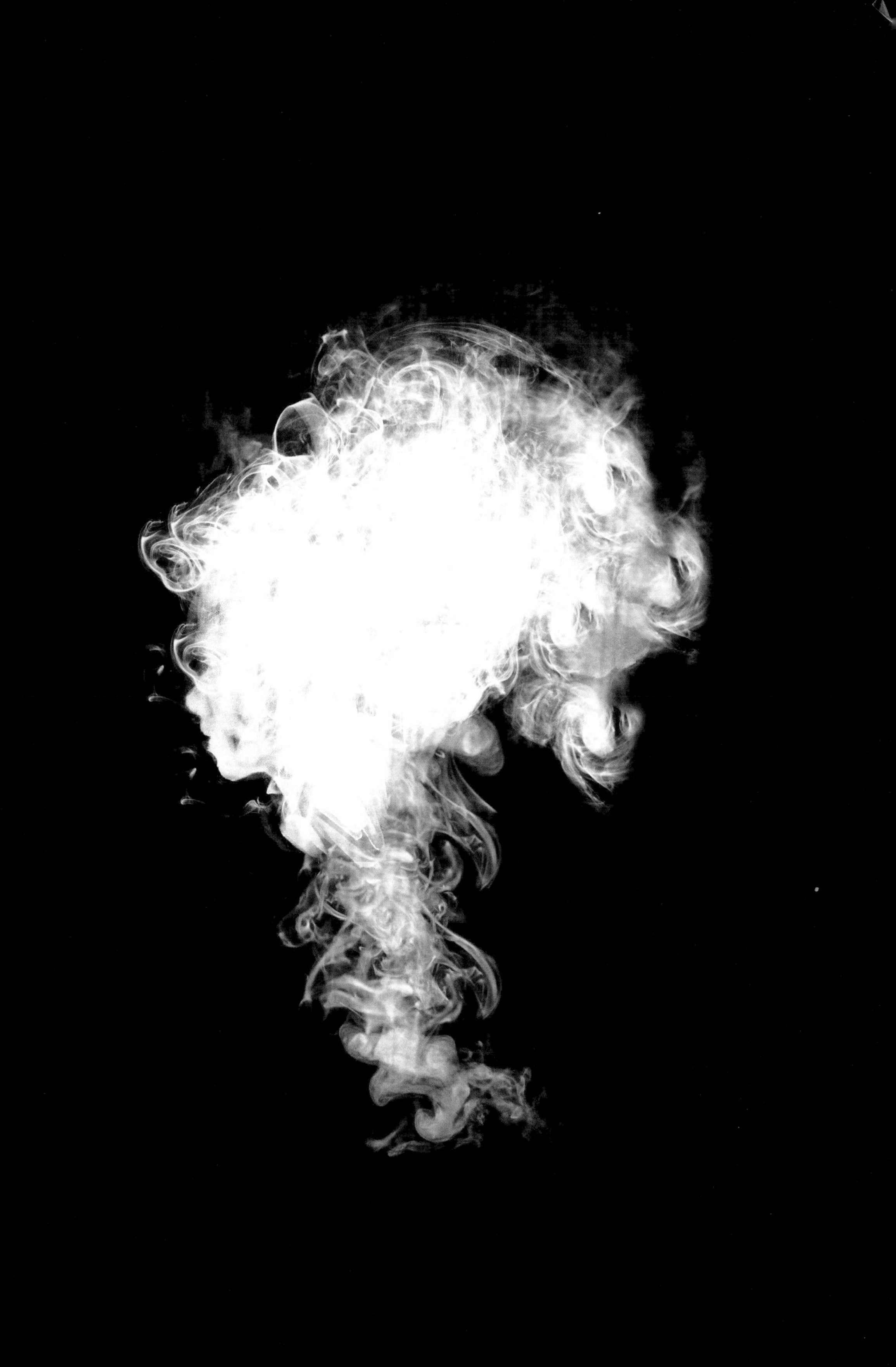

HART OF THE MATTER

STORY: DAVID F. WALKER
ART: MARK MD BRIGHT
COLORS: TOYIN AJETUNMOBI

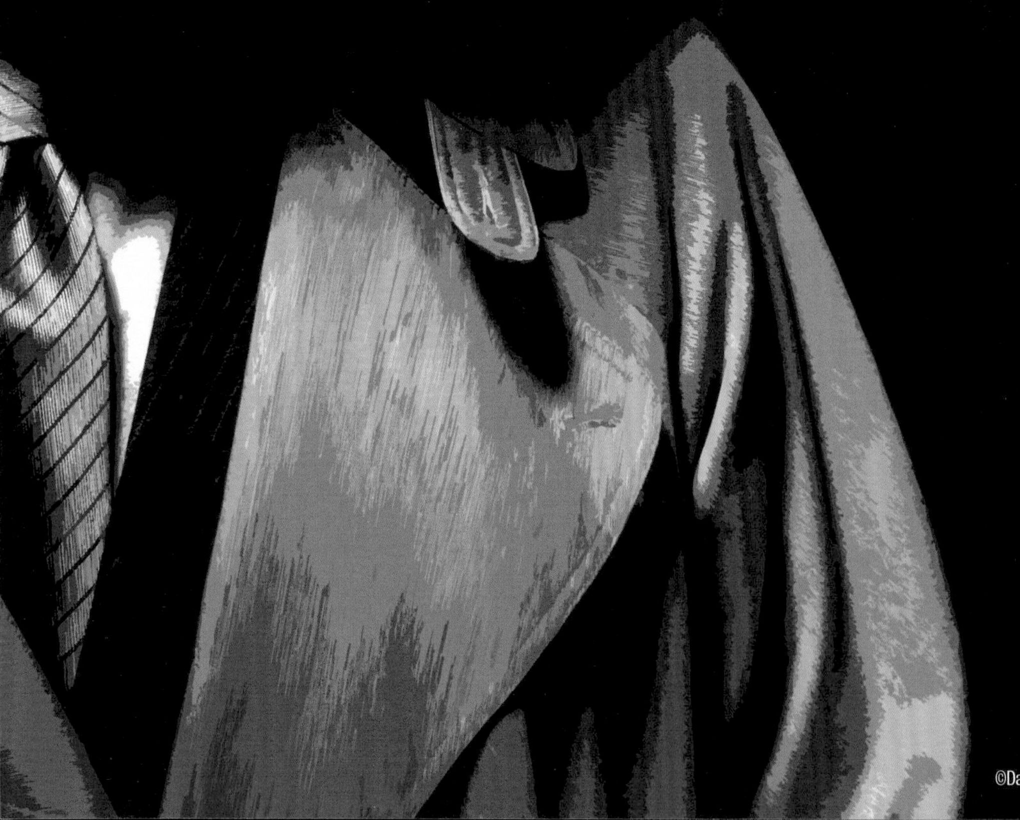

GHETTO AVENGER
SISTER OF SIN
MR. FENTON JAMES, OWNER AND PUBLISHER OF VERITAS PUBLISHING, HAS DEDICATED HIS LIFE TO PUBLISHING BOOKS FOR "PEOPLE WHO MOVE THEIR LIPS WHEN THEY READ."
VERITAS' BOOKS DON'T MAKE BEST-SELLERS LISTS, BUT THEY ENTERTAIN READERS, AND FENTON JAMES TRIES TO TREAT HIS WRITERS FAIRLY AND WITH RESPECT.
STILL, THE PUBLISHER OF SUCH BOOKS AS "THE GHETTO AVENGER" AND "SISTER OF SIN" DRAWS THE LINE...
BOBBY, I'M SORRY, BUT I'M NOT GIVING YOU ANOTHER DIME UNTIL YOU FINISH THE NEW MANUSCRIPT.
AND THAT, MY FRIEND, IS THAT.
WITH MORE THAN TWELVE BOOKS TO HIS CREDIT, BOBBY HART IS THE MOST PROLIFIC AND POPULAR WRITER WORKING FOR VERITAS. HE IS ALSO DESPERATELY IN NEED OF CASH.
ROW
COME ON, YOU KNOW I'M GOOD FOR IT, FENTON.
IF I GIVE YOU MONEY IT WILL JUST GO UP YOUR ARM. IT ALWAYS GOES UP YOUR ARM.
AS YOUR FRIEND AND PUBLISHER, GET BACK TO WRITING. STAY AWAY FROM THE SMACK.
NOT ANYMORE. I'M CLEAN, MAN.

HALF WAY THROUGH HIS NEW BOOK, BOBBY FINDS HIMSELF IN A DESPERATE SITUATION.
THE PERFECT WORDS ELUDE HIM. HIS DREAMS ARE HAUNTED BY HIS EXPERIENCES DURING THE WAR IN VIETNAM. HE NEEDS SOMETHING TO SOOTHE HIS TROUBLED MIND AND SPARK HIS IMAGINATION.
SHOES
HOTEL
IT'S A DANGEROUS KIND OF INSPIRATION AND SOOTHING ...PAID FOR IN CASH AND INJECTED INTO A VEIN.
SORRY, CAN'T HELP YOU, MY MAN.
UNFORTUNATELY, THERE'S NEVER ENOUGH MONEY TO QUIET SOME DEMONS...
ARE YOU OUT YOUR MIND?!
YOU STILL OWE ME FROM LAST TIME, FOOL.
...FORCING BOBBY TO MAKE PROMISES HE'S LIKELY TO NEVER KEEP.
THIS AIN'T NO CHARITY WARD, MAN.
YOU GOT THREE DAYS TO GET ME MY BREAD, AND DON'T MAKE ME COME LOOKIN' FOR YOU.

CREATIVITY COMES EASY FOR SOME WRITERS...

...WHILE OTHERS STRUGGLE WITH IT.

HE KNOWS THAT HE'LL NEVER WRITE THE GREAT AMERICAN NOVEL, AND BOBBY HART IS FINE WITH THAT.

HE WRITES FOR GUYS WHO DRIVE BUSES AND HAUL TRASH.

HE WRITES FOR PEOPLE WORKING THE ASSEMBLY LINE, AND ALL THE BROTHERS DOING HARD TIME. AND THEY ALL LOVE HIS BOOKS.

BOBBY HART WRITES OF THE HUSTLERS AND HEROES HE NEVER GOT AROUND TO BEING.
GHETTO AVENGER
ALRIGHT, BABY...

TIME TO MAKE SOME MAGIC.

Killing came easy for Curtis Freeman.
CLIK
CLAK
CLIK
CLAK

With revenge on his mind and pair of .45s in his hands, he'd torn the city apart looking for the gang of dope-peddling scum.
CLIK
CLAK
CLIK
CLAK

And neither God nor the Devil gave a shit about such things.

CLIK CLAK

CLIK CLAK

CLIK CLAK

It all came down to this moment.
CLIK CLAK CLIK CLAK

Some men begged, while others fought back.
CLIK CLAK

CLIK CLAK CLIK CLAK

CLIK CLAK CLIK CLAK

Sometimes the lion's prey bites and claws for its life.
CLIK CLAK CLIK CLAK

Not that he thought of himself as a lion, it was just that Curtis Freeman…
CLIK CLAK NOK NOK NOK

MOTHERFU...
WHO IS IT?
NOK NOK NOK

GO AWAY!
I'M WORKIN'!
NOK NOK NOK

NOK
NOK
NOK

I GAVE YOU THREE DAYS...

...AND I TOLD YOU NOT TO MAKE ME COME LOOKIN' FOR YOU.

MAN, JUST ANOTHER FEW DAYS. I'M ALMOST DONE, THEN YOU'LL GET YOUR MONEY.

BLAM

CREATIVITY COMES EASY FOR SOME WRITERS...

...WHILE OTHERS STRUGGLE WITH IT.
THE END.

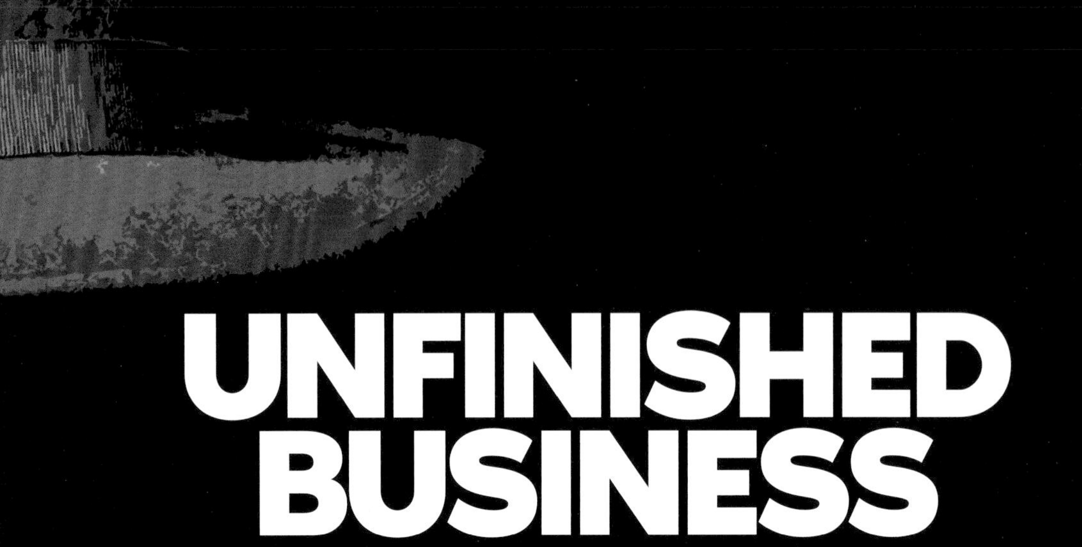

UNFINISHED BUSINESS

STORY: GREG ANDERSON ELYSÉE

ART: GUILE WITH ERIC VAN ELSLANDE

COLORS: TOYIN AJETUNMOBI

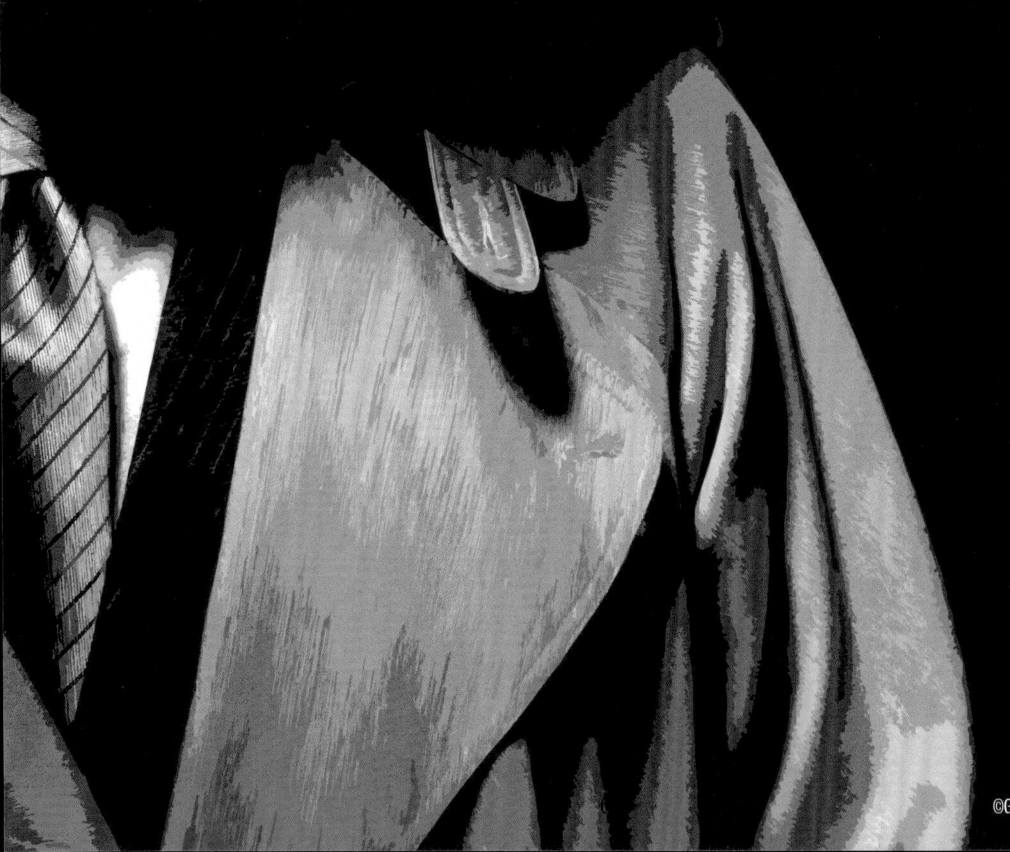

IT'S BEEN WEEKS SINCE I'VE HAD A CASE. I'M GRASPING FOR AIR, HOPING FOR SOMETHING--ANYTHING--TO FALL OUT OF THE SKY AND INTO MY LAP. ANYTHING...
NEED MY MEDS... NO MEDS EQUAL STRESS... NO STRESS MANAGEMENT... ANXIETY. THAT'S THE NAME FOR IT. SHIT GOT ME FEELING UNHINGED... LIKE I'M A DIFFERENT PERSON...
BREATHE... IN... OOOOUT...
ONE. TWO. THREE. FOUR. FIVE...
KNOCK KNOCK KNOCK
A CASE?! SHIT, I HOPE SO... PLAY IT COOL, DON'T MAKE YOURSELF SOUND DESPERATE...
COME IN!
WELL... GOOD EVENING, SIR...
HOT DAMN IS ALL THAT COMES TO MIND RIGHT NOW.
ALTHOUGH I WANT TO LAUGH AT HIS HAIR... WHO EVEN DOES THAT ANYMORE?
YET IT HAS A CHARM TO IT COMING FROM HIM... HEH... IT'S ALL IN THE SWAG, LACK OF A BETTER TERM. WHAT AN AWFUL TERM.
DETECTIVE JAMES MORT?
HE IS ME. YOU HAVE ME AT A DISADVANTAGE.
ROBERT DUBOIS. A PLEASURE, DETECTIVE.
PLEASURE IS ALL MINE.
WHAT CAN I DO YOU FOR-- I MEAN, WHAT CAN I DO FOR YOU? PLEASE. SIT.
SMOOTH, JAMES. REEEAAAL SMOOTH.

...
UH. YOU GOOD?
...
PARDON? OH. MY APOLOGIES.
I TEND TO LOSE MY PLACE SOME TIMES.
IS IT HIS FULL LIPS THAT HE LICKS TO KEEP HIS WORDS AS SMOOTH AS HIS MIDNIGHT SKIN? OR IS IT HIS EYES THAT AUTOMATICALLY WARRANTS MY FULL AND UNDIVIDED ATTENTION?

HOLD UP. IS HE... FLIRTING WITH ME?

BUT YES... I HAVE A BIT OF A SITUATION. SOMEONE VERY DEAR TO ME IS MISSING. I NEED YOU TO FIND HIM.
SOMEONE DEAR TO YOU? WHO IS HE TO YOU?
JUST A DEAR FRIEND. I WAS TOLD THAT YOU'RE QUITE GOOD IN MISSING PERSONS' CASES. I FEAR I MAY NEVER SEE HIM AGAIN.
ALRIGHT. DO YOU KNOW THE LAST PLACE HE WAS?

YES. TULSA. THAT'S WHERE I NEED YOU TO GO AND FIND HIM, MY DEAR FRIEND.
I'M SORRY, WHAT? YOU KNOW TULSA IS HUNDREDS OF MILES AWAY FROM HERE.
IS THIS SOME KIND OF JOKE? PLENTY OF P.I'S IN TULSA, I'M SURE.

YES, BUT ONLY ONE JAMES MORT. COME OOON, I'VE BEEN LOOKING FOR YOU FOR SUCH A LONG WHILE...

I'LL MAKE IT WORTH YOUR WHILE.
SO, DETECTIVE MORT. HOW SOON CAN YOU START?
HOLY HELL...

TULSA
ROUTE 66
THE THINGS I DO FOR MONEY AND A PRETTY FACE...
TULSA, OKLAHOMA... QUITE THE HISTORY THIS TOWN HAS. ONCE WIPED OUT OF THE HISTORY BOOKS, PEOPLE ARE FINALLY STARTING TO BECOME FAMILIAR WITH THE INFAMOUS MASSACRE...

WOULD HAVE LOVED TO HAVE SEEN WHAT BLACK WALL STREET LOOKED LIKE.

DID A BACKGROUND CHECK ON THIS ROBERT DUBOIS... EVERYTHING CHECKS OUT AND HE'S LEGIT. MONEY WENT THROUGH, HENCE THIS NICE ASS HOTEL...
HOT

THIS FRIEND OF HIS, THOUGH... JOHN R. LANGSTON... NOW HE'S A MYSTERY. ONLY THING I CAN FIND CLOSE TO THIS CHARACTER IS JOHN RAINEY LANGSTON... DIED 1921... DURING THE GODDAMN MASSACRE.
DID DUBOIS SEND ME ON SOME TYPE OF WEIRD ASS CHASE? THAT MOTHERFUCKER COULD HELP IF HE'D ANSWER HIS FUCKING PHONE!
DAMN IT. BREATHE, BOY. YOU GOT AND TOOK YOUR MEDS, YOU'RE GOOD...

ONE. TWO. THREE. FOUR. FIVE... YOU GOOD...
RELAX, MAN. TAKE A WALK.

BEEN COOPED UP IN THE CAR FOR A WHILE AND THOSE WALLS WERE CLOSING IN...
GET A FEEL OF THE AREA BEFORE GOING GUNS BLAZING INTO YOUR WORK, YOU PARANOID BUZZKILL.

HEY!

WHAT THE HELL?
EENY, MEANY, MINY, MOE!

CATCH A NIGGER BY THE TOE!

BLAM

WHAT--
WHAT IS GOING ON?
BLAM
UGHH!
AIIEEEE!
OH MY GOD!

UGHH UHH UHH GASP UGHH

HEY, HEY! IT'S ME, IT'S ME! STAY WITH ME, ALRIGHT? YOU'RE OKAY! YOU'RE FINE...
ROB--
ROBERT?

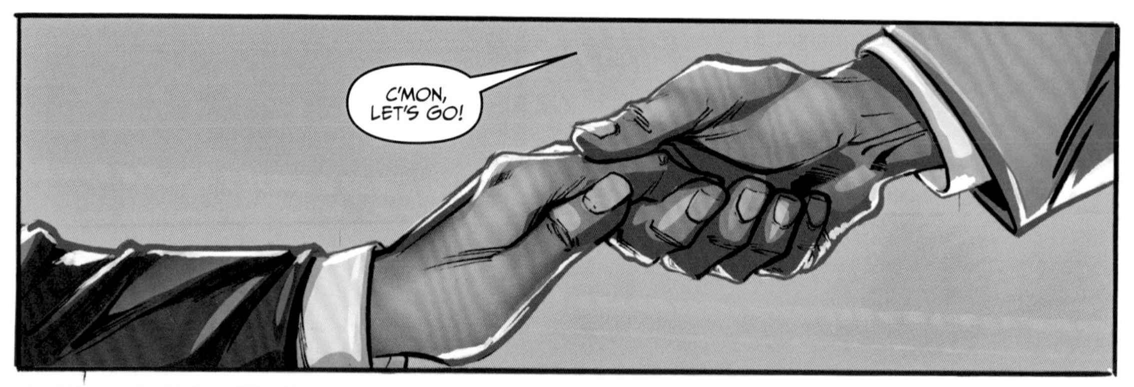
C'MON, LET'S GO!

WHAT IS HAPPENING?! I WAS JUST SHOT!

SHHH, IT'S OKAY.
R-- ROBERT?
I'M... LANGSTON...?

YOU REMEMBER? RAINEY? MY RAINEY.

BUT... HOW? OH, MY GOD. ROBBIE.
IT'S YOU, RAINEY.

MY HEAD... I HAVE ALL THESE THOUGHTS AND MEMORIES... I'M JAMES... BUT ALSO JOHN RAINEY LANGSTON... AM I...
...A REINCARNATION?
SEE? I KNEW YOU WERE A SMART DETECTIVE.
AND YOU?

BABY, I'M ON UNFINISHED BUSINESS. I'M AN ANCESTOR. JUST LIKE EVERYONE ELSE HERE.

NO... AFTER WE WENT DOWN TO THE STATION WHEN THEY TOOK RICK ROWLAND. AND ALL HELL BROKE LOOSE.
THEY CAME DOWN OUR STREETS, GUNS BLAZING. AND THEY GOT ME.

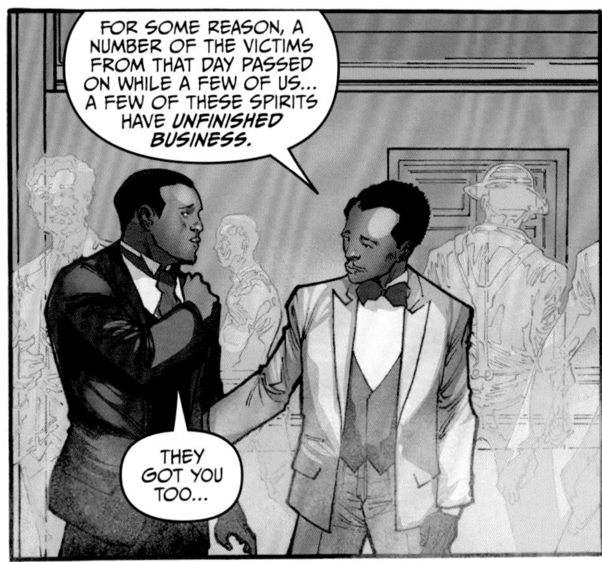
FOR SOME REASON, A NUMBER OF THE VICTIMS FROM THAT DAY PASSED ON WHILE A FEW OF US... A FEW OF THESE SPIRITS HAVE ***UNFINISHED BUSINESS.***
THEY GOT YOU TOO...

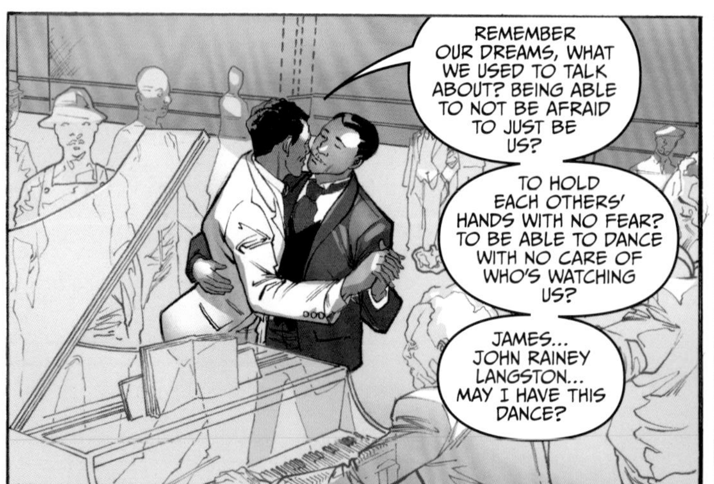
REMEMBER OUR DREAMS, WHAT WE USED TO TALK ABOUT? BEING ABLE TO NOT BE AFRAID TO JUST BE US?
TO HOLD EACH OTHERS' HANDS WITH NO FEAR? TO BE ABLE TO DANCE WITH NO CARE OF WHO'S WATCHING US?
JAMES... JOHN RAINEY LANGSTON... MAY I HAVE THIS DANCE?

YES, YOU MAY, ROBERT DUBOIS.

GUESS I SHOULD MAKE MYSELF COMFORTABLE?
WHO'S NEXT?

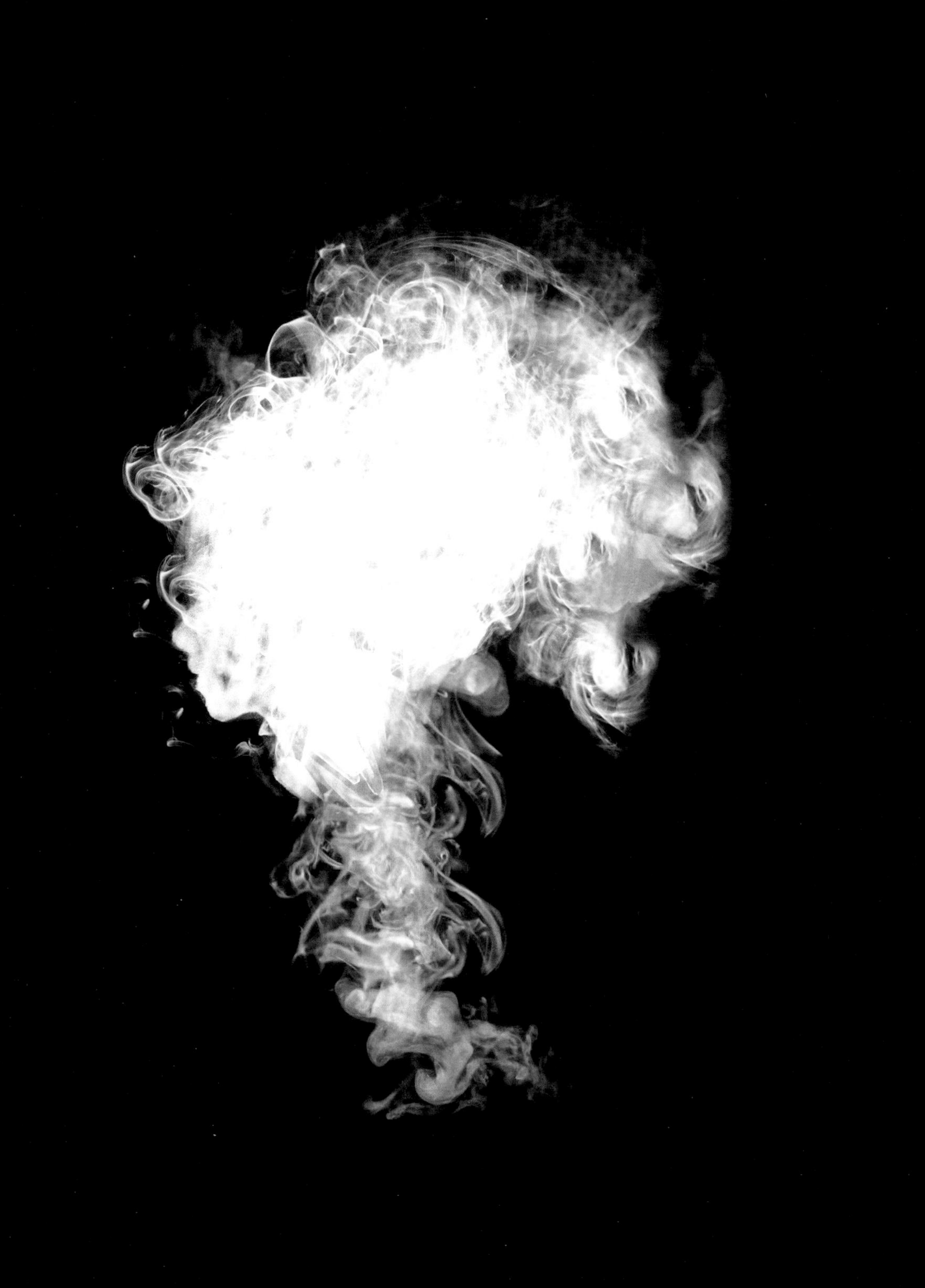

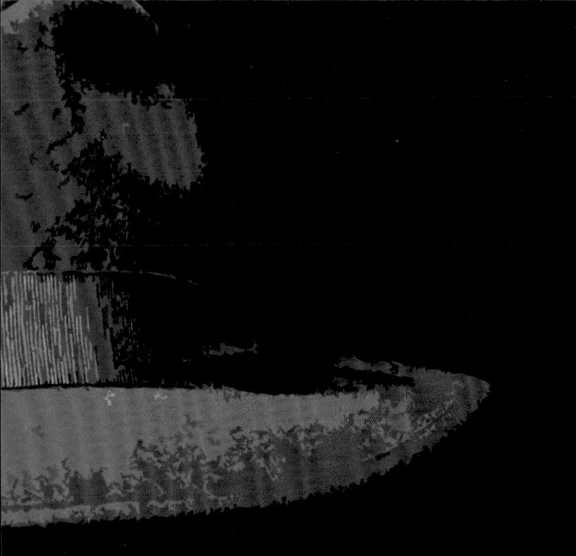

ENTANGLEMENT

STORY: ERIKA HARDISON ART: KAREN S.DARBOE
COLORS: WALT BARNA

CHICAGO, 1991.
I WASN'T EXPECTING TO SEE THE BOSS OF THE SOUTH SIDE'S BRAINS ON THE FLOOR. THIS MURDER LOOKS PERSONAL.
AN UPCOMING SINGER WORKING HERE HIRED ME TO LOOK INTO THE REGAL'S ACTIVITIES SO HERE I AM.

HEY, YOU SHOULD GO NOW.
SOMETIMES I MISS BEING A COP, THEN I REMEMBER HOW MANY COPS ARE *CROOKS.*
I MIGHT NOT HAVE A BADGE ANYMORE, BUT I'LL ALWAYS FIND A WAY TO PROTECT OTHERS.

THAT'S SWEET HIPS. SHE LOOKS MORE LIKE A GANGSTER THAN A FAMOUS JAZZ SINGER.

AND THERE'S DAMITA, SHE'S THE HOTTEST *NEW JACK SWING* ACT IN TOWN RIGHT NOW.

DAMITA HIRED ME TO SEE IF SHE WAS BEING SHORT-CHANGED BY THE REGAL.
I COULDN'T SAY NO TO MY FIRST LOVE...

IT WAS ONLY A FEW WEEKS AGO WHEN DAMITA CAME TO MY OFFICE TO TELL ME HER CONCERNS.
ME AND SWEETS MIGHT NOT BE SAFE AT THE REGAL.
YOU THINK YOU AND YOUR MOM ARE IN DANGER?
MORE GOONS ARE COMING TO THE CLUB AND SHE WANTS BOSS MAN TO MAKE HER CO-OWNER IN THE EVENT SOMETHING GOES DOWN.

HIRE ME. I'LL PROTECT Y'ALL.
...BUT ESPECIALLY *YOU*...

BUT NOW...
ALRIGHT, WHAT SHOULD I BE SEEING OR BETTER YET, NOT SEEING?

AWW SOOKIE, SOOKIE NOW!

'SUP BONES! GOOD LOOKS ON LINKING UP.
WORD. SAM, YOU'RE THE ONLY ONE WHO CAN GET ME TO MEET AT A CRIME SCENE.
SAM, IS THE REGAL CLOSED FOR GOOD?
I DON'T KNOW BONES, EVERYTHING IS IN THE AIR RIGHT NOW.
I HAVE SOME POWERFUL FRIENDS IN HIGH PLACES SO IF YOU KNOW HOW BOSS MAN DIED, YOU SHOULD TELL ME.
I AIN'T NO SNITCH. WE COOL, BUT YOU STILL 5-O.

I WORK FOR MYSELF THESE DAYS AND IF YOU NEED PROTECTION, I GOT YOU.
YOU GOT ME?
SCOFFS
YOU DON'T HAVE ANY IDEA WHAT YOU'RE GETTING INTO.
SO TELL ME.
IF THEY KNEW I WAS TALKING TO YOU, THEY'D THROW ME IN LAKE MICHIGAN.

SO IT'S "THEY", HUH?
YEAH, "THEY"
LOOK, IF YOU WANT SOME INFO, GO RAP WITH DJ PYNK HOUSE AT WNJS.
AIGHT BET. WE SHOULD PROBABLY SNEAK OUT THE BACK.

THOSE TLC GIRLS ARE GOING TO BE THE NEXT BIG THING! DON'T FORGET YOU HEARD IT HERE FIRST!
WE ABOUT TO PAY THESE BILLS SO MAKE SURE YOU HIT MY HOTLINE AFTER THESE MESSAGES ON THE OTHER SIDE!
AS I WAS GETTING READY TO LEAVE, I HEARD A LOT OF COMMOTION IN THE STATION'S HALLWAY.

I HEAR YOU KNOW THE DEMO ON EVERYBODY.
YOU WERE AT THE REGAL WHERE BOSS MAN WAS FOUND DEAD.
YOU HEARD ANYTHING?
EVERY OLD G HAS ITS DAY.
NOTHING IS GUARANTEED, EXCEPT FOR BLOOD AND GREEN.
IF YOU NEED A CLUE INSTEAD, LOOK FOR THE HOT FOX DRESSED IN RED.
DON'T GET TOO CLOSE, CUZ SHE MIGHT SLIT YOUR THROAT.

HEY, WHERE'S MY DJ! EX-DETECTIVE. LOOKING FOR SOMETHING.
I JUST WANTED SOME JANET TICKETS.
DON'T YOU HAVE A CASE TO IGNORE OR A CAT TO RESCUE FROM A TREE?
WOW. SHOTS FIRED--
PEACE IN THE MIDDLE EAST.

JUST MIND YOUR OWN BUSINESS AND STAY AWAY FROM MY DAUGHTER.
DON'T NEED HER AROUND FAILURES.
SHE'S A STAR. YOU'RE WAY OUT OF YOUR LEAGUE.
AS SWEETS WAS THREATENING ME, I COULDN'T HELP BUT NOTICE SHE WAS MISSING A VERY EXPENSIVE DIAMOND EARRING.

DAMITA WAS PAGING SO I TOLD HER TO MEET ME AT MY BUILDING. SHE WAS WAITING FOR ME DOWNSTAIRS.

BOOM
DAMITA!

I SNATCHED HER BRAIDS WITH MY HANDS TO PUT THE FIRE OUT. AS SOON AS WE GOT UPSTAIRS, THE PHONE RANG.
WHAZZUP, TALK TO ME.
AYE CHRIS, I GOT THE AUTOPSY REPORT AND I FOUND A RELATIVE OF THE DECEASED.
MY PLUG CONTINUED TO GIVE ME MORE INFO AND NOW I HAVE EVERYTHING I NEEDED TO SOLVE THIS CASE.

ARE YOU OK?
NO, I CAN'T BELIEVE SOMEONE TRIED TO KILL US.
DON'T WORRY, THIS IS GOING TO END ONCE AND FOR ALL.
I KNEW WHAT I HAD TO DO.
AND IT DIDN'T TAKE MUCH TO GET EVERYONE TO SHOW UP AT THE CLUB.

THE PERSON WHO KILLED BOSS MAN IS IN THIS ROOM.
I KNEW WHAT I WAS GETTING MYSELF INTO AND I CAME PREPARED.

EVERYONE HERE HAD A MOTIVE TO KILL BOSS MAN.
DJ PYNK...

...BOSS MAN WAS BLACKMAILING YOU TO PLAY HIS GOON'S MUSIC ON THE RADIO.
HE ALSO PAID OFF YOUR DJ EQUIPMENT.
AYE MOMMA, WHY THE DRAMA. AIN'T NO KILLIN' JUST TOP BILLIN'.

BONES, YOU HATE SWEETS AND I DON'T BLAME YOU. SHE'S A BULLY.
SWEETS, I... I NEVER SAID THAT!
YOU'D DO ANYTHING SHE TELLS YOU TO DO. EVEN MURDER.

DAMITA, YOU KNEW BOSS MAN WAS YOUR FATHER AND YOU RESENTED HIM FOR NEVER TAKING CARE OF YOU LIKE HE SHOULD HAVE.
I KNEW BUT I WOULD NEVER OFF HIM! YOU HAVE TO BELIEVE ME, SAM!

SWEETS, WHEN I FIRST SAW YOU WITH THE COPS, IT WAS CLEAR YOU KNEW THEM.
AFTER I DEVELOPED MY PICTURES, IT WAS CLEAR A COP PASSED YOU SOMETHING SHINY.
AT THE RADIO STATION YOU ONLY WORE ONE EARRING.
YOU DON'T WEAR BOTH EARRINGS BECAUSE YOU BROKE A PIECE OF THE SETTING OF YOUR EARRING AND GETTING IT FIXED WOULD EXPOSE YOU AS A MURDERER.

YOU GOTTA LOT OF NERVES, LITTLE GIRL.
I TOLD YOU TO STAY OUT OF GROWN FOLKS' BUSINESS!
WELL, THIS IS IT...
BULLS 23

FBI. SURRENDER NOW.
WHOOMP, THERE IT IS.

COME OUT WITH YOUR HANDS UP!
BLAM

I THOUGHT I HAD HER CORNED IN THE KITCHEN.

BLAM

NOBODY CAN STOP ME NOW.
I'M THE BIGGEST BOSS IN THE CHI.
NOBODY CAN STOP SWEET HI--

WHEN I LOOKED UP, I SAW DAMITA CRYING AND WE BOTH SAW SWEETS FALL, TOO.
SHE HAD ALSO BEEN SHOT.

YOU KILLED YOUR OWN MOMS.
SHE WAS STRAIGHT UP EVIL. I DON'T WANT THIS LIFE. YOU'RE ALL I NEED.

PLEASE TELL ME YOU'RE GONNA BE OKAY?
HI-FIVE

AS LONG AS I GOT YOU, I WILL BE.
Fin

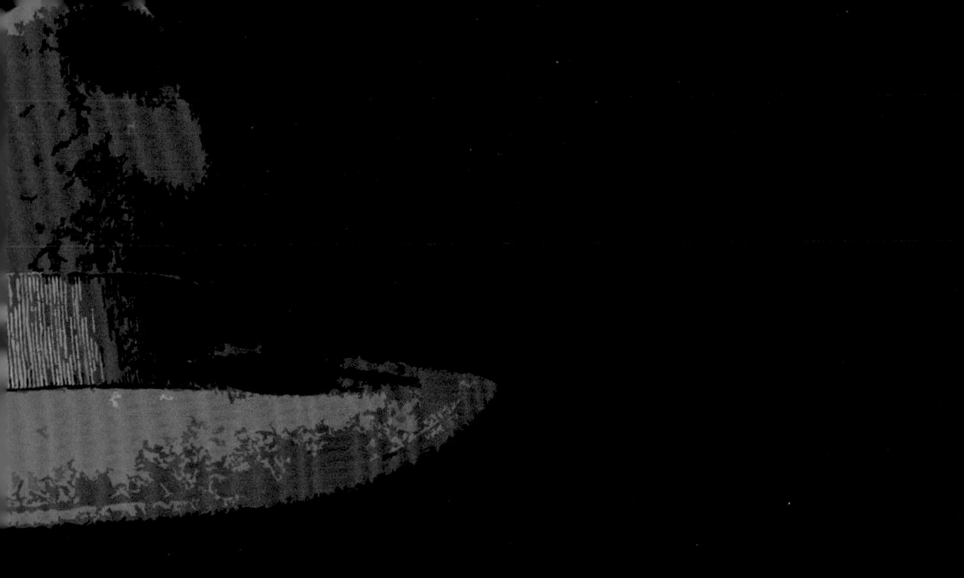

GLUTTONY

STORY: DORPHISE JEAN AND VLADIMIR ALEXIS
ART & COLORS: WALT BARNA

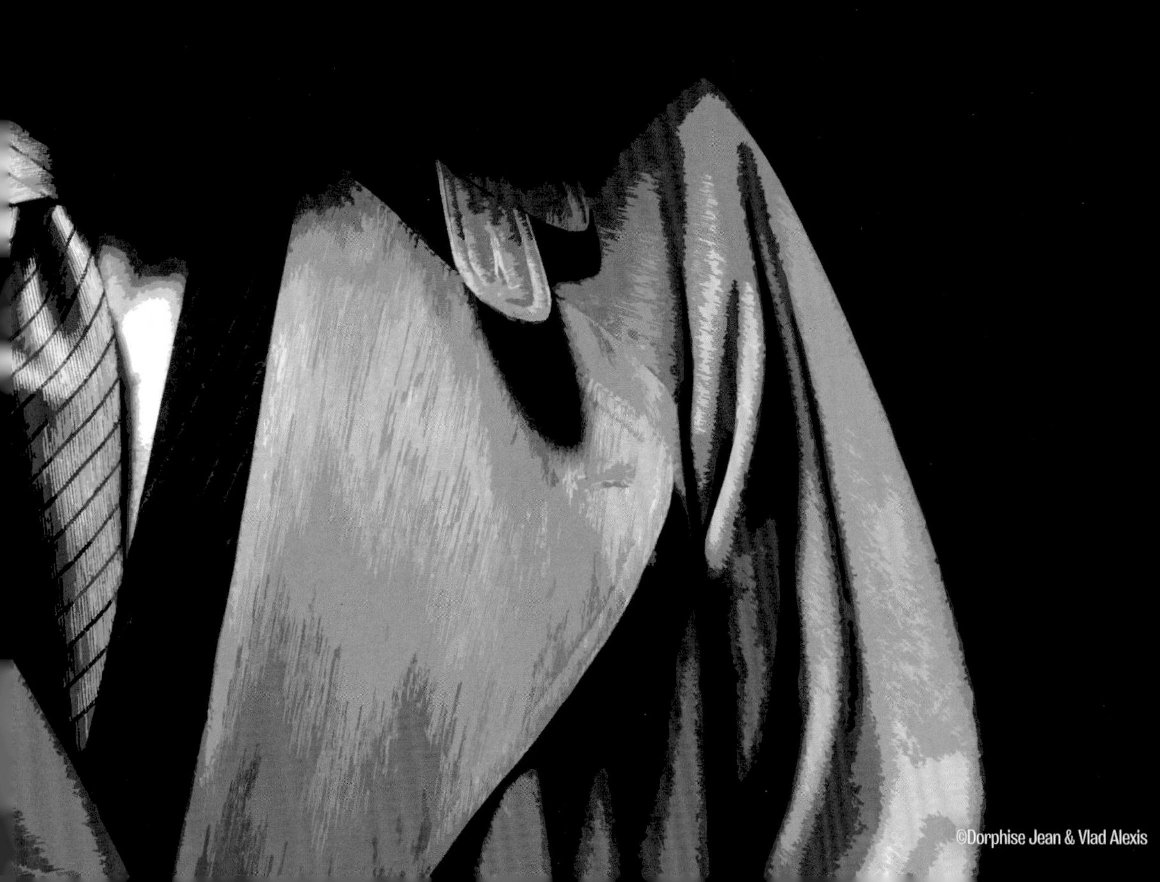

Presidential Candidate Rutherford Grimes' House
Miami, FL
AHHHHH
WHAT THE F@#*?
IS EVERYTHING OKAY SIR?
NO. THERE'S A FREAKING GOAT HEAD IN MY BED.
MAKE SURE THE ROOM IS CLEAR. AND GET THAT THING OUT OF THE ROOM.
FIND THE BASTARDS WHO DID THAT AND BURY THEM UNDER TIFFANY'S ROSE BED!
I'M SURE SHE AND THE ROSES WOULD APPRECIATE THE FERTILIZER.
YES, SIR. DON'T WORRY. WE'LL FIND THE PERPETRATORS ASAP.

Grimes Campaign HQ.
Hours Later.
SIR, WE RAN THE CAMERAS BACK OVER 50 TIMES. WE COULDN'T FIND ANYONE ENTERING OR EXITING THE PROPERTY.
SO THE GOAT JUST MAGICALLY APPEARED IN MY BED. IS THIS WHAT YOU'RE TELLING ME?
OF COURSE NOT, SIR.

UFFF
WE ARE DEALING WITH A STRATEGIST. THEY TARGETED GRIMES FOR A REASON, BUT THE QUESTION IS WHY.

WHY WOULD YOU MAKE AN ASSUMPTION LIKE THAT?
FOR FUCK'S SAKE, LITTLE HAITI IS IN OUR DISTRICT. I DON'T NEED TO CONTINUE SPELLING IT OUT, DO I?
MAKING FALSE ASSUMPTIONS LIKE THAT IS VERY DANGEROUS.
PUFF
HAAAH
LOOK. WE HAVE TO FACE THE FACTS. IT'S HIGHLY PROBABLE THAT SOMEONE PLACED A CURSE ON HIM.

WHAT DID YOU JUST SAY?
SIR, WE NEED TO CONTINUE THE INVESTIGATION BEFORE WE JUMP INTO CONCLUSIONS.

RUTHERFORD, WE'VE KNOWN EACH OTHER FOR A WHILE. BELIEVE ME WHEN I TELL YOU YOU'D RATHER HAVE A HORSE HEAD. THAT THERE ISN'T A WARNING.
WHY WOULD SOMEONE WANT TO PUT A HEX ON ME?
I AM A GOOD LEADER. PEOPLE LOVE ME. LOOK AT EVERYTHING THAT I ACCOMPLISHED.
WELL, THERE'S ONE WAY TO FIND OUT.

Botanica Little Haiti, Miami, FL
BOTANICA
OPEN
ARE YOU SURE IT'S HERE, JOHNSON?
100% POSITIVE, SIR. MY INFORMER NEVER FAILED ME BEFORE.
EMERGENCY EXIT ONLY
O BONDYE TOUPISAN MWEN MANDE W ED OU AK YON DEMANN.
<OH MIGHTY GOD I ASK YOU TO ASSIST WITH A REQUEST.>
DONNEZ-MOI LE POUVOIR, JE VOUS EN SUPPLIE!
<GIVE ME THE POWER, I BEG YOU!>
POU M JWENN REPONS JEN GASON SA A AP CHACHE A.
<TO FIND THE ANSWERS THAT THIS YOUNG MAN SEEKS.>
POU MIZERIKÒD NANM MWEN.
<TO THE MERCY OF MY SOUL>
DONNEZ-MOI LE POUVOIR, JE VOUS EN SUPPLIE!
<GIVE ME THE POWER, I BEG YOU!>
AHH... OU KRAZE ZO DE TWA MOUN WI!
<YOU HAVE BROKEN A FEW PEOPLE!>
WHAT DO YOU MEAN I HAVE BROKEN A FEW PEOPLE.
SA K POU PEYE GEN POU L PEYE.
<RETRIBUTION SHALL BE HAD.>
THIS WAS JUST SOME SICKO, I'M RUTHERFORD FRIGGING GRIMES.
VRÈ MECHAN AN GEN POU L BAY TÈT LI.
<THE TRUE VILLAIN WILL REVEAL ITSELF.>

WHAT HAPPENED? ARE YOU OKAY?
EMERGENCY EXIT ONLY
I'M FINE, I THINK...
Back at the HQ
WHAT IS THIS NOW?
IT WAS DELIVERED WHILE YOU WERE GONE, SIR. WE COULDN'T TRACK THE SENDER.
rd Grimes
The enemy is always the one you show the most support for.
Greed over empathy.
It doesn't take a spell to reveal the real monster.
BURN THIS SHIT!

Grimes Home.
"...IT'S QUITE PROBABLE SOMEONE PLACED A CURSE ON HIM."
CLICK
PUFF PUFF
THIS CAN'T BE... I BURNED THOSE BOXES! THIS IS CRAZY.
LUB DUB LUB DUB LUB DUB
YOUR OPULENT WAYS HAVE FORCED SUFFERING ON MANY.
HAH HAH HAH HAH
EXCUSE ME MA'AM, DO I KNOW YOU?
SA KA RIVE OU PA SONJE M WI, POUTAN.
<YOU MAY NOT REMEMBER ME, HOWEVER.>
M KONN KIYES OU YE.
<I KNOW WHO YOU ARE.>
OU SE MAJISTRA A, EGOYIS OU AK ARIVIS OU FIN DEPAFINI LAVI NOU!
<YOU ARE THE MAYOR. YOU RUINED OUR LIVES WITH YOUR GREED AND SELFISHNESS>
OU ABIZE KONFYANS NOU, OU PWOFITE KE N TE NAYIF.
<YOU ROBBED US OF OUR TRUST AND TOOK ADVANTAGE OF OUR NAIVETY.>
OU VÒLÈ TOUT RESOUS KI TE KA BAY NOU EDIKASYON, OU TRAYI NOU!
YOU TOOK AWAY RESOURCES FOR OUR EDUCATION, YOU SOLD OUT!
NO!

WHAT DO YOU WANT FROM ME? ARGHHH!
LEAVE ME ALONE.
I'M SORRY, I'M SORRY.
BREAKING NEWS!
TUNE IN AT 7PM ON WSVN WHERE WE DISCLOSE THE INVESTIGATION UNDERWAY ABOUT PRESIDENTIAL CANDIDATE GRIMES EMBEZZLEMENT SCHEME ON THE MIAMI/LITTLE HAITI PROPERTIES.
MRS. GRIMES.
MR. JOHNSON.
I HOPE THERE'S CHAMPAGNE. 'CAUSE I LOVE WHEN A PLAN COMES TOGETHER.

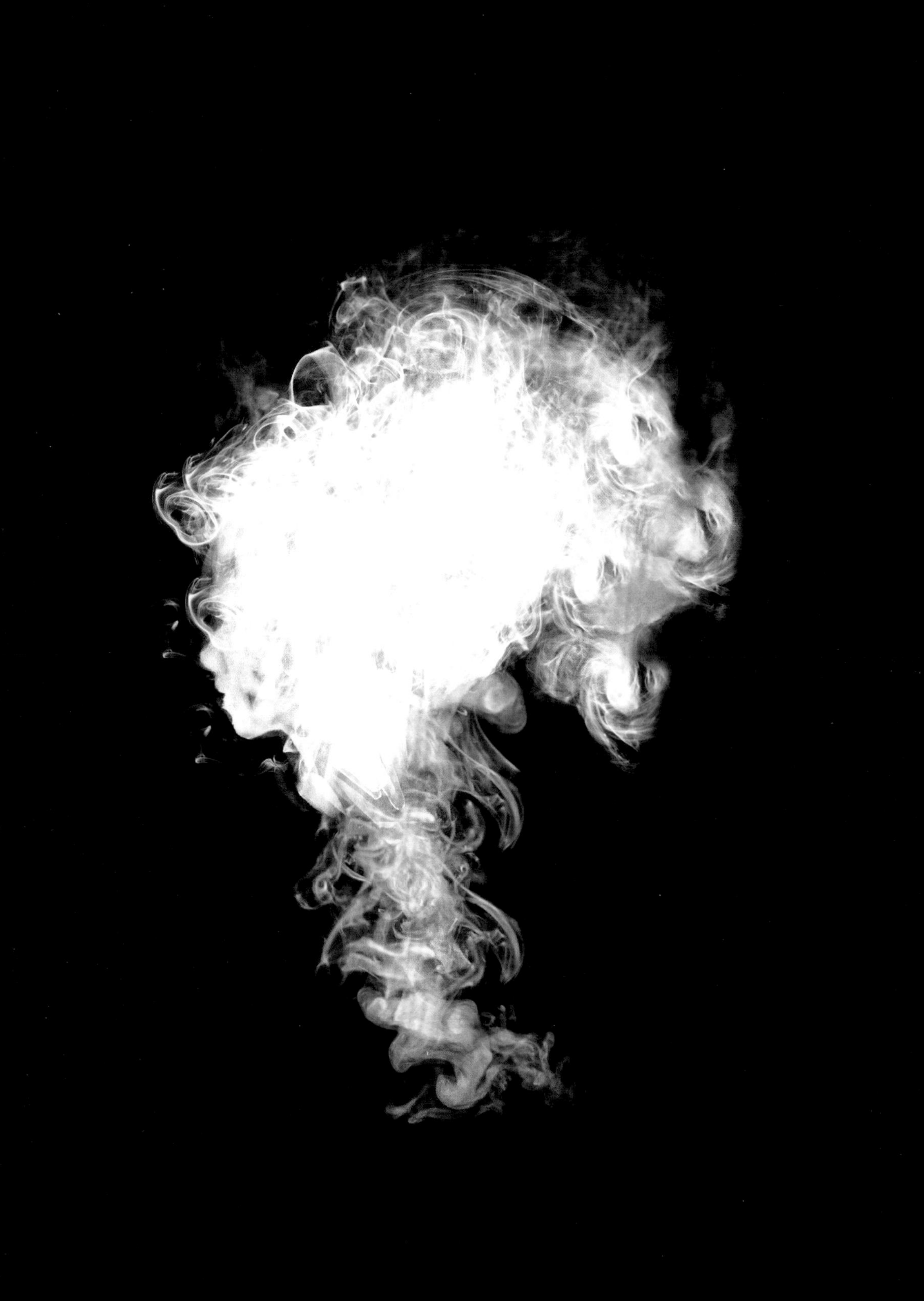

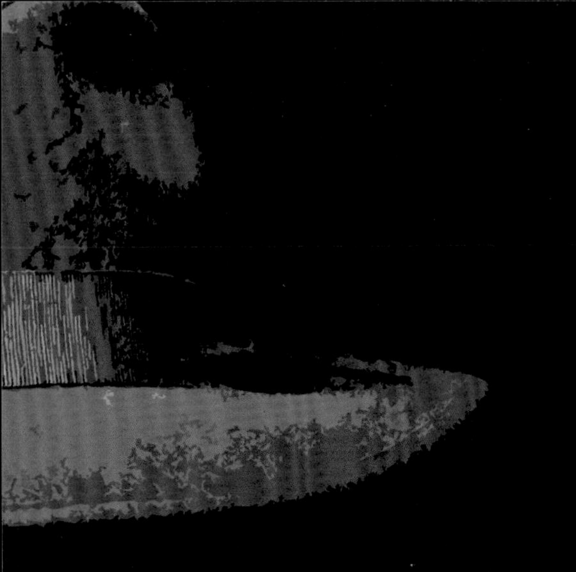

NERU

STORY: MD MARIE

PENCILS: DON WALKER

INKS: LARRY WELCH • COLORS: TOYIN AJETUNMOBI

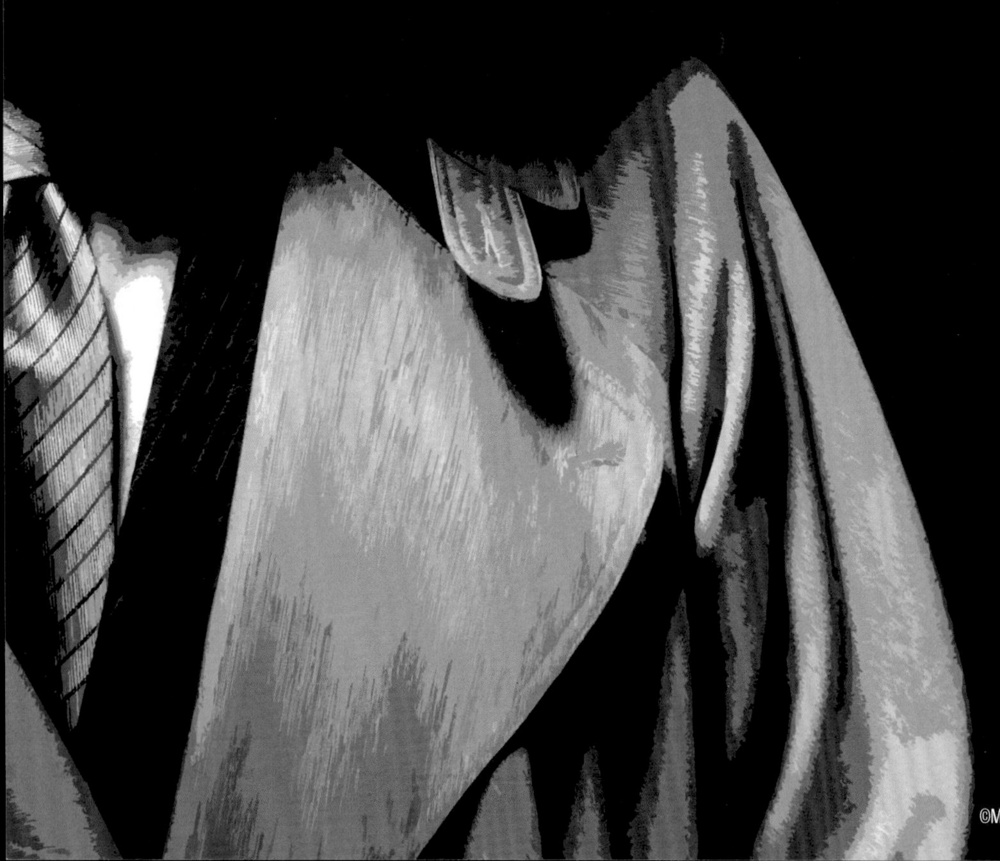

Virginia.
2065/05/06. 0300 hours.
SAMSARA: THE CYCLE OF DEATH AND REBIRTH.
STRONG... SMART... SOLDIER... DEAD WOMAN.

SO EASILY DELETED.

NEITHER MOURNED NOR MISSED.

FIRST THE MURDER OF MY BODY...
DISCOUNTED IN LIFE. DELETED IN DEATH.

I STARE AT THE IMAGE OF MY REMAINS LYING DEAD ON THE CLIFFSIDE. FROM AN ACCIDENT??
WHY CAN'T I REMEMBER?! THERE'S NO WAY I DID THIS!

THEN THE ASSASSINATION OF MY SOUL...
HOW MANY TIMES CAN YOU STEAL MY HUMANITY?!!

Washington D.C.
2065/05/06. 0600 hours.
CAPTAIN NERU! MEETING'S OVER. THE GENERAL WANTS YOU DEBRIEFED.
THEN DEBRIEF ME.
YOU'VE BEEN GREENLIT FOR OPERATION JUSTICE.
IS THAT...
NOT HERE.

...AND FINALLY, THE EXTERMINATION OF MY DIGNITY.
I KNOW WHERE YOU WERE. YOU HAVE TO STOP OBSESSING!
I CAN'T HELP IT. I *KNOW* I WAS MURDERED!
I WAS GETTING OUT! I WAS ABOUT TO BE FREE!
...AND THEN YOU DIED! I KNOW! WE'VE BEEN OVER THIS!

LAST TIME MY CHIP WAS DAMAGED, I REMEMBERED SOMETHING.
I MANAGED TO ARCHIVE IT BEFORE I WAS SHUTDOWN.
I DON'T KNOW WHAT I'M LOOKING AT.
IT'S A MEMORY! IT'S HIM! I KNOW...
FROM WHEN?! WHOSE MEMORY?! WHO'S "HIM"??

I DON'T KNOW! BUT I KNOW THIS HAS TO DO WITH...
YOUR OBSESSION IS GOING TO GET YOU REPROGRAMMED!
YOU MEAN MURDERED! AGAIN!
I'M SO SORRY CAP. IT'S MY FAULT.
NO. I SHOULD'VE READ THE FINE PRINT.
DR. KASI SAID YOU WERE DIFFERENT...

I KNEW THAT IF YOU DIED...
THAT I WOULD NEVER BE FREE?
I THOUGHT THEY'D JUST AUTOPSY YOU... OR HARVEST ORGANS. NOT... THIS.

Pentagon.
2065/05/06. 1100 hours.
WITH ALL DUE RESPECT GENERAL, KEEPING HER FILE FROM...
SHE DIDN'T EVEN GET A PROPER FUNERAL.
RUIZ! STAY FOCUSED!
HOW SHE DIED IS NOT IMPORTANT!

WHY WOULD WE WASTE MONEY BURYING AN ORPHAN??
DOESN'T EVERY SOLDIER DESERVE A FUNERAL, SIR?

THERE'S NO ONE TO EVEN VISIT THE GRAVE!
SHE WAS. NOW SHE'S A MALFUNCTIONING WEAPON.
SHE WAS A PERSON SIR.
YOU NEED TO MAKE HER FORGET ABOUT THAT NONSENSE!

YOU NEED TO CONVINCE HER THAT IT WAS AN ACCIDENT.
HER KNOWING WILL CHANGE NOTHING. SHE'S STILL PENTAGON PROPERTY.

RUIZ! FOR THE RECORD, I DON'T LIKE HER BEING THERE EITHER.

DR. KASI HERE!
WHY IS SHE STILL INVESTIGATING HER M...
HER ORGANIC BRAIN CANNOT BE OVERRIDDEN.
IF SHE REMEMBERS, NONE OF US WILL BE SAFE!
I'LL TAKE CARE OF IT TONIGHT.

FLASHES OF MY PAST ARE LIKE BLIPS ON A SCREEN.
WHHHHIIIIR
UPLOAD TO DRONE DRIVES AND FIREWALL COMPLETE. DETACHING FROM NEURAL NETWORK.

DRONE DETACHED AND VIGILANT. RECORDING IN PROGRESS.
IT'S JUST YOU AND ME NOW.

DR. ARDEN KASI. MONSTER, HACKER, AND MADMAN. POSSIBLY MURDERER.
VRRRR
DRONES DEACTIVATE. ALL SYSTEMS DOWN. COMMENCE TOTAL SYSTEM RESET.

VRRRR
TONIGHT, I'M THE HACKER. MY DRONE STAYS ONLINE. I SEE, HEAR, AND DOWNLOAD EVERYTHING.
SOME WORK AND THEN LOTS OF PLAY.

HE IMPRISONED ME IN THIS CYBERNETIC TOMB! MADE ME HIS EXPERIMENT, HIS PROPERTY...
GASP!!
SOON, YOU'LL BE MY GOOD LITTLE SOLDIER GIRL AGAIN.

THANKFULLY, YOU WEREN'T COMPLETELY UNSALVAGEABLE. YOU. ARE. MINE!
THIS ENDS TONIGHT, ASSHOLE.

SYSTEM OVERRIDE INITIATE! SAFETY PROTOCOL ENGAGE! SOMETHING WORK!!

THE ASSASSINATION OF MY SOUL AND EXTERMINATION OF MY DIGNITY IN ONE STRIKE!
YOUR REAL BODY WAS SO...
...YOU RUINED EVERYTHING! BITCH!!
NOW YOU CAN'T LEAVE! UUUUHHHH!
MOBILITY RESTORED. PALM SENSORS CHARGED.

YES! SCREAM BASTARD! YOUR DEATH GIVES ME LIFE!
...AND SET TO LETHAL.
AHHHHHH!!! STOP IT! NOOOOO!!!
AAAAAAAHHHHHHH!!!

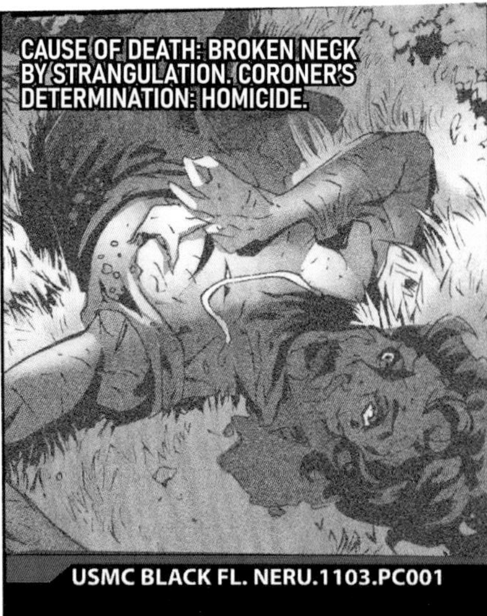

THE BEGINNING.

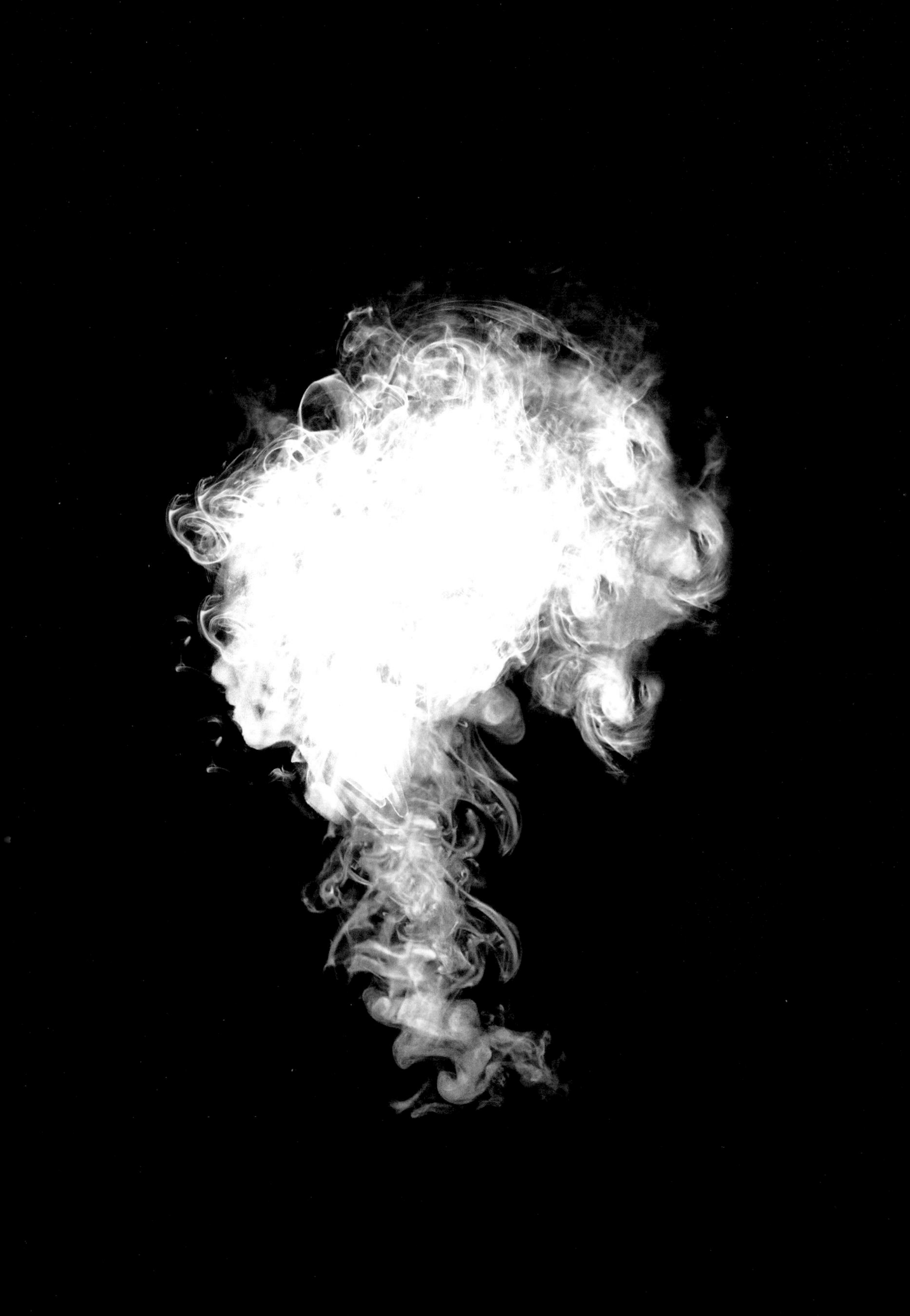

THE CIRCUIT

STORY: TROWA CHRISTOPHER HARRIS
ART: DAVID BRAME

DUKE'S PLACE 2:30AM
WHAT'S THE WORD ON THE LATEST SUPPLY OF GREENS?
I HATE SPADES.
AHEAD OF SCHEDULE, SATCH. THEY'VE BEEN UPDATED FROM THE INTEL WE GATHERED FROM THE MIDWEST.
I ESPECIALLY HATE NIGHTS LIKE THESE WHEN THE LOSER HAS TO "CLEAN UP", ESPECIALLY WHEN IT AIN'T MY MESS.
OPERATIONS ARE RUNNING SMOOTHLY OVER AT THE REPUBLIC.
WE'LL BE READY TO RECEIVE AND DISTRIBUTE ACROSS THE MID ATLANTIC WITHIN THE MONTH.
WE SHOULD HAVE ZERO PROBLEMS BY THE TIME OF HIS ARRIVAL IN SPRING.
REDD HAS YOUNG RAYMOND RUNNING THE ODDS AND ENDS IN ORDER TO KEEP UP APPEARANCES.
RAY?
OUTTA SIGHT! HOW IS DEEK AND THE BOY? MORE IMPORTANTLY, WHAT DOES THE KID KNOW?
DEEK'S BOY...
PATTIE'S BOY. JUST AS HOT-HEADED AS HIS FATHER, BUT HE'S A GOOD KID.
HE'S OUTTA THE LOOP AND KNOWS NOTHING OF OUR DEALINGS.
LOOKS LIKE TONIGHT JUST WASN'T YOUR NIGHT REDD!
SHIT...
LET'S GET THAT FINE OFFICER OVER THERE WHERE HE BELONGS.
OH, AND MR. BROWN, PLEASE TAKE CARE OF THE REST.
FURTHER MISTAKES WON'T BE RESOLVED OVER CARDS, UNDERSTOOD?
YESSIR. I'LL GET THIS CLEANED UP
I MADE YOU A PROMISE.
ONE I INTEND TO KEEP.
THIS LIFE KEPT ME FROM YOU, AND EVENTUALLY TOOK YOU FROM ME. THE PATH I WALK, IS ONE THE BOY WILL NEVER FOLLOW.

DUKE'S PLACE
BACK ALLEY
3:30 AM
PSH..A PROMISE. WHAT A FOOL I AM.
A PROMISE IS NO DIFFERENT THAN THIS OFFICER'S BONES.
EASILY BROKEN, WHEN PUT UNDER ENOUGH STRESS.
THERE'S NOTHING YOU COULD HAVE DONE FOR THEM THAT NIGHT, REDD...
...YOU'VE GOT TO LET IT GO, BROTHER.
THEY DESERVED BETTER...SHE DESERVED BETTER.
THAT BOY SHOULD STILL HAVE A MOTHER...
WE NEVER SHOULD HAVE TAKEN OUR EYES OFF OF THEM.. THAT'S ON ME.
WE'LL FIND THEM.
ALL OF THEM.
BUT FOR NOW, WE NEED YOU TO FOCUS.
WE HAVE A FAR MORE PRESSING MATTER THAT REQUIRES YOUR ATTENTION
NO REST FOR THE WEARY I SEE. ANOTHER THREAT TOWARDS BROTHER M'S ARRIVAL?
PERHAPS, BUT THERE'S A MORE PERSONAL MATTER I NEED YOU TO HANDLE AS WELL.
I HAVEN'T SPOKEN TO DEEK IN YEARS. LAST TIME...WASN'T PLEASANT.
HOW THE HELL DO YOU EXPECT ME TO GET THIS TO HIM, CAB?
I'M THE LAST MAN HE'D EVER WANNA SEE, ESPECIALLY NOW.
LIKE I SAID, A PERSONAL MATTER.
SISTER E FACILITATED THE TRANSFER OF PATTIE'S FUNDS FROM CHICAGO, TO THE INDUSTRIAL BANK. THAT CHECK? THAT'S MY OFFERING.
BEST TO KEEP SATCH OUT OF THE LOOP ON THIS ONE, FOR OBVIOUS REASONS. SHE WAS ONE OF US, REDD.

I KNOW.. IT'S JUST..
...LISTEN, LOOKING OUT FOR THAT BOY ALSO MEANS LOOKING OUT FOR HIS FUTURE.
THE LEAST WE CAN DO IS MAKE SURE RAY AND DEEK ARE CARED FOR.
PHILIP
YEAH MAN, I DIG...NOW, WHAT ABOUT THE OTHER JOB?
DUE TO MR.BROWN'S CARELESSNESS, THERE'S A NEW PLAYER ON THE BOARD THAT PRESENTS A THREAT TO US.
HE'LL BE YOUR DRIVER FOR TONIGHT. FIND OUT WHAT YOU CAN.
MR.BROWN, WHY DON'T YOU GET YOURSELF ACQUAINTED WITH REDD.
YOU TWO ARE GOING TO TAKE A LITTLE TRIP AND HAVE A CHAT
REDD, I'LL TRUST YOUR JUDGMENT.
NO SWEAT.
ASSHOLE
SO YOU'RE THE COMEDIAN, HUH?
HEARD ABOUT YOU OUT ON TOUR. YOU DON'T SPEAK MUCH, DO YOU?
ROY *ROCKIN'* BROWN".
HEARD ABOUT YOU TOO..
MAYBE YOU SHOULD SPEAK ***LESS***.
EVER HEARD THE ONE ABOUT LOOSE LIPS SINKING SHIPS?
WRONG PLACE, WRONG TIME. IT WASN'T THAT COP'S NIGHT. SHOULDN'T HAVE TAILED ME.
IF YOU DON'T WANT YOUR NEXT SINGLE TO BE *ROCKIN' IN THE POTOMAC*, I'D SHUT UP AND HEAD WEST.
WHATCHA GOT THERE?
A STORY ABOUT A SHIP.
THAT'S TAKING ON WATER...
"AGENT FOWLER IS HEREBY AUTHORIZED TO CONTINUE HIS INVESTIGATION INTO AN ORGANIZATION KNOWN ONLY AS 'THE CIRCUIT' -- J. EDGAR HOOVER"

BROOKMONT DAM
THE CIRCUIT KNOWS YOU TALKED.
COLD OUT HERE THIS MORNING.
GROWING UP, MINISTER TOLD ME ABOUT NOAH ONCE. HOW GOD FLOODED THE EARTH TO WASH AWAY THE SINS OF MAN...

MAYBE THAT'S KINDA WHAT WE'RE DOING EVERY TIME WE DRIVE OUT HERE.
I WONDER WHEN IT'LL BE MY TURN IN A BARREL. RIGHT ABOUT NOW, I BET ROY IS ASKING HIMSELF THAT SAME QUESTION.
THAT'S CRAZY! YOU THINK I'D SELL US OUT?!
SAMMY JACKSON SURE DID, AND TO THE FEDS.

NO CONNECTIONS, ROY.
YOU THINK WE WOULDN'T FIND OUT ABOUT YOUR "MANAGER"?

SAMMY... NO...
HIS LOOK TELLS ME EVERYTHING I NEED TO KNOW

HE WAS LIKE A FATHER...ALL WE TALKED ABOUT WAS MUSIC...
IT'S EVERYTHING TO HIM... I DON'T KNOW HOW THIS HAPPENED, I SWEAR I NEVER TOLD HIM ABOUT US!
CAB TOLD YOU TO KILL ME, DIDN'T HE?!
LISTEN, THE ONLY REASON YOU'RE NOT IN THAT BARREL BEHIND YOU, IS I KINDA BELIEVE YOU.
CAB TOLD ME TO FIND OUT WHAT YOU KNOW. LUCKY FOR YOU, THAT'S SQUAT. WHAT HAPPENS NOW IS UP TO THE BOARD, AND WHAT WE FIND OUT FROM SAMMY.

WHEN WE FIND HIM.
LET ME HELP FIX THIS!

SO THAT'S IT? JUST GONNA LEAVE ME HERE FOR ANOTHER TRIGGER MAN? YOU SAID YOU BELIEVED ME!
CLOSE THE DOOR, ROY.
IT'S LATE, I'M BEAT AND I COULD REALLY USE A DRINK.

HE'S PROBABLY SHITTING HIS PANTS. HE DESERVES IT.
I PROMISE...
I'LL MAKE THIS RIGHT!!!!!!
ROY BROWN IS MANY THINGS, BUT HE'S NOT A TRAITOR. MISTAKES CAN BE MADE, ESPECIALLY IN OUR LINE OF WORK. THE SECRETS WE CARRY AND LIES WE TELL, EASILY EXPOSED AFTER A FEW SHOTS OF GIN.
ONE MISTAKE CAN COST YOU YOUR LIFE.

LONG WAY FROM WASHING DISHES BACK IN BRONZEVILLE.
SWALLOWED A BAR OF SOAP ONCE TO AVOID THE WAR. DIDN'T TAKE WELL TO THE THOUGHT OF DEATH THEN. BUT NOW? WHAT AM I DOING, PATTIE?
REDD'S APARTMENT 5:31 AM
COULD HAVE SAVED A COUPLE OF BUCKS AND SET ME UP AT THE HOTEL BY THE REPUBLIC, BUT THE CIRCUIT IS ALL ABOUT APPEARANCES.
AT LEAST THEY KEEP IT STOCKED.

I CALL THE REPUBLIC TO UPDATE CAB ON WHAT I FOUND BEFORE CHUGGING DOWN A BOTTLE OF NEAREST WHISKEY.
GOING OVER THE FILES SHOWS ME HOW LITTLE THE FBI KNOWS. THAT'S GOOD FOR ROY.

A SAFEHOUSE, NOW OCCUPIED BY HOP HEADS. WE HAVEN'T BEEN THERE IN MONTHS. A PAGE FROM AN OLD GREEN BOOK... SHIT... I'M DRIFTING OUT, AND YOU'RE COMING FOR ME AGAIN...

AREN'T YOU, PATTIE...
I WANT A FAMILY, REDD. YOU CAN LEAVE WITH ME... I'M GOING TO MARRY DEEK. I'M HAVING A BABY... I DON'T KNOW... I'LL BE BACK IN CHICAGO FOR A FEW DAYS. CAN WE TALK?
KILL!
PLEASE HELP ME, MINISTER... MY MOMMA GOT HURT.

KILL!
KILL THEM ALL REDD... KILLKILLKILL!
KILL!
NO!
KILL!
KILL!
KILL!
1865

THE PHONE SAVES ME FROM MY BOOZE INDUCED HELL.
RRRRING

CAB CALLS ME TO HEAD OVER TO 2B. CAN'T BE TOO GOOD FOR ROY.

I'LL SEND OFF THE DRIVER AND TRY TO WALK IT OFF. THIS IS GOING TO BE A BAD NIGHT.
SEE YOU LATER, PATTIE.

REPUBLIC 6:01 PM
I'M NOT REALLY A MOVIE GUY, BUT THE PLACE HAS ITS CHARMS.
THEATRE HAS BEEN UNDER THE CARE OF THE CIRCUIT SINCE ITS RENOVATION ALMOST 30 YEARS AGO...
I REMEMBER WHEN I FIRST GOT ASSIGNED HERE TELLING CAB I KNEW NOTHING ABOUT RUNNING A THEATRE.
FOREVER THE SHOWMAN, HE TOLD ME THAT THE BEST SHOW IN THE HOUSE WOULDN'T BE FOUND ON SCREEN.

THE STORAGE CELLAR TAKES YOU A BLOCK WEST TO THE LINCOLN THEATRE. A GIFT FROM OUR FOUNDERS.
RIGHT TO THE DOOR OF A HIDDEN SPEAKEASY. THE CREW CALL IT 2B
REDD, MY BOY!
THE PLACE WAS A BLAST DURING THE PROHIBITION DAYS. AVERAGE JOE'S, COPS, POLITICIANS, ALL LAUGHING AND DANCING THE NIGHT AWAY. MY KINDA SCENE... AT LEAST THAT'S WHAT HE TELLS ME...
YOU LOOK TERRIBLE, YOU NEED TO GET YOURSELF SOME REST.
GOT PLENTY, SATCH, NOW WHAT'S THE SKINNY ON THESE POOR BASTARDS?
IT WOULD SEEM MR.BROWN WAS QUITE BUSY WHILE YOU WERE UH, INDISPOSED TODAY.

MEET SPECIAL AGENT FOWLER AND SAMMY JACKSON!
THEY'VE BEEN IN TOWN SINCE MR.BROWN ARRIVED LAST WEEK.
SEEMS MR. BROWN WANTED TO HANDLE THAT ONE PERSONALLY.
HE'S JUST A LITTLE LATE FOR THE CURTAIN CALL.
WAS IT ROY WHO TUNED THEM UP TOO?
Still make a deal...

SOMETHING HAS ALWAYS MADE MY SKIN CRAWL AROUND THE OLD MAN. SOMETHING ABOUT THAT SMILE, AND HE'S ENTIRELY TOO CLEAN...

PLEASE G...
YOU SHOULDN'T BE HERE, SATCH.
JUST LEAVING MY BOY...
...I WAS JUST HERE FOR THE OPENING ACT, AND THE SECOND IS ABOUT TO START.

EVERYBODY KNOWS PAIN. SOME MORE THAN OTHERS. OVER TIME, YOU BUILD UP A TOLERANCE, BUT IT HURTS ALL THE SAME.
WHY SAMMY?
PAIN COMES IN MANY DIFFERENT FLAVORS. I THINK OUR PEOPLE COULD WRITE THE BOOK ON ALL OF THEM.
NU..NOW WAIT! LET ME EXPLAIN, BOY!!!
THE FUCKING FEDS?! DO YOU KNOW WHAT YOU'VE DONE?!!
TONIGHT, ROY IS EXPERIENCING ONE OF MY LEAST FAVORITE FLAVORS.
I CAN EXP...
BETRAYAL.
I GOT POPPED PLAYIN' THE NUMBERS BY FOWLER *COUGHS* CUT ME A DEAL.. I'M SORRY, KID.
I DIDN'T KNOW A THING... FOWLER ALREADY HAD HIS EYE ON YOU. THAT MONEY. THE CARS... LOOKED SUSPICIOUS. SO I FOLLOWED YOU ONE NIGHT...
...FIGURED YOU'D BRING ME INTO THE HUSTLE BUT YOU NEVER DID! YOU KNEW WE WERE STRUGGLING!
I TOLD YOU I'D FIX THIS, REDD.
NO MORE STRUGGLING, SAMMY. CRYSTAL AND JOE WILL BE CARED FOR.
SON, PLEASE! JUST LET ME GO...YOU DON'T HAVE TO...
BETRAYAL DOESN'T DISCRIMINATE. THE BETRAYED CAN ALSO BECOME BETRAYERS, CREATING A VICIOUS CYCLE THAT CAN RIP YOU APART...
LEAVING YOU, HOLLOW...
REDD...WHAT WE DO NEXT WON'T COME EASY, BUT AS PROMISED, I HAVE A LEAD INTO WHAT HAPPENED THAT NIGHT.
YOU REMEMBER PAUL MITCHELL, DON'T YOU? TURNS OUT, HE SOLD US OUT.
THEATRE OWNER? YEAH..I REMEMBER HIM...
IF ONLY IT WERE THE WORST...

BETRAYAL HAS A COUSIN THAT HURTS JUST AS MUCH.
THAT COUSIN'S NAME IS REGRET.
TALKED ABOUT PAIN ONCE WITH JOE LOUIS BACK IN CHICAGO AFTER THE CESAR BRION FIGHT.
INTEL POINTS TO MR. MITCHELL'S CONNECTION TO A MAN MATCHING RAY'S DESCRIPTION AT THE THEATRE THAT NIGHT.
WE ALSO DISCOVERED A WIRE TRANSFER ON THE NIGHT OF...
...REDD, HE WAS AN AFFILIATE...
...I'M SO SORRY.
WHAT?!
YOU TOLD ME THEY WERE SAFE!
HOW DID YOU NOT FUCKING KNOW?
HE TOLD ME SOMETHING THAT HAS BECOME THE GOSPEL ABOUT PAIN.
Let's not be rash! I've helped you people before..you've got this all wro...
IT'S THE HITS YOU DON'T SEE COMING THAT HURT THE MOST.
WHO...
WHO DO YOU WORK FOR?
WHO KILLED HER?!
THOK THOK THOK
REDD STOP!!! HE'S THE ONLY LEAD WE'VE GOT!!!
THOK THOK THOK THOK THOK
YOU SOLD THEM OUT, MITCHELL...
WAIT! Ledger... Back at the theatre.. Safe in my office. Chauvin! Town sheriff paid me to...
FOR PATTIE.
MITCHELL IS THE FIRST TO FALL. LIKE A MODERN DAY JUDAS, HE SOLD US OUT FOR SILVER. WELL MITCHELL, I HOPE THE 30 PIECES OF SILVER WERE WORTH IT. HERE'S 8 MORE.
I MADE A PROMISE TO KILL EVERY BASTARD RESPONSIBLE FOR WHAT HAPPENED TO YOU THAT NIGHT AND PROTECT YOUR BOY.
A PROMISE.
I INTEND.
TO KEEP.
The End?

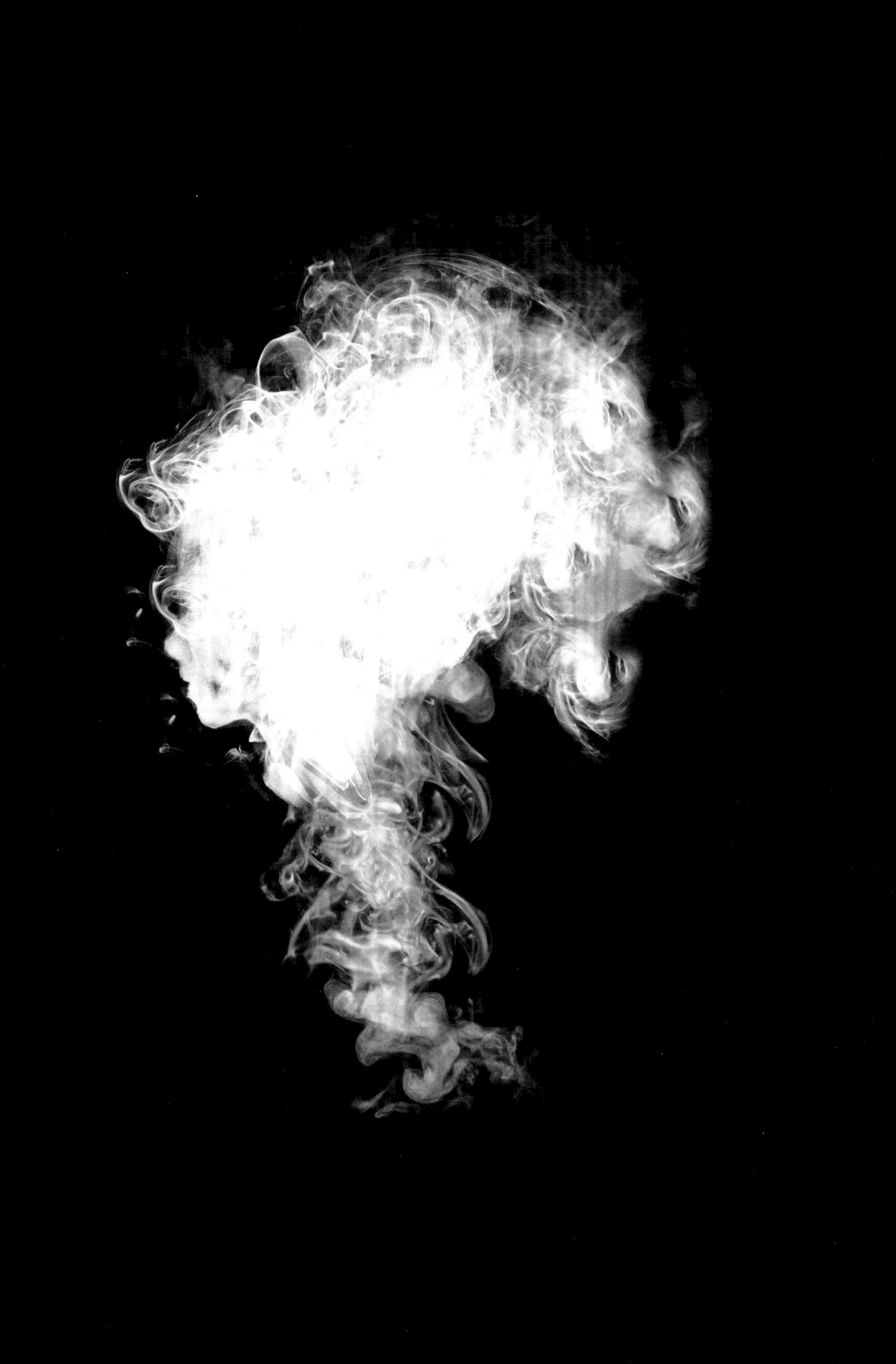

CHASING THE NIGHT

STORY: HANNIBAL TABU ART: QUINN MCGOWAN

COLORS: PARIS ALLEYNE

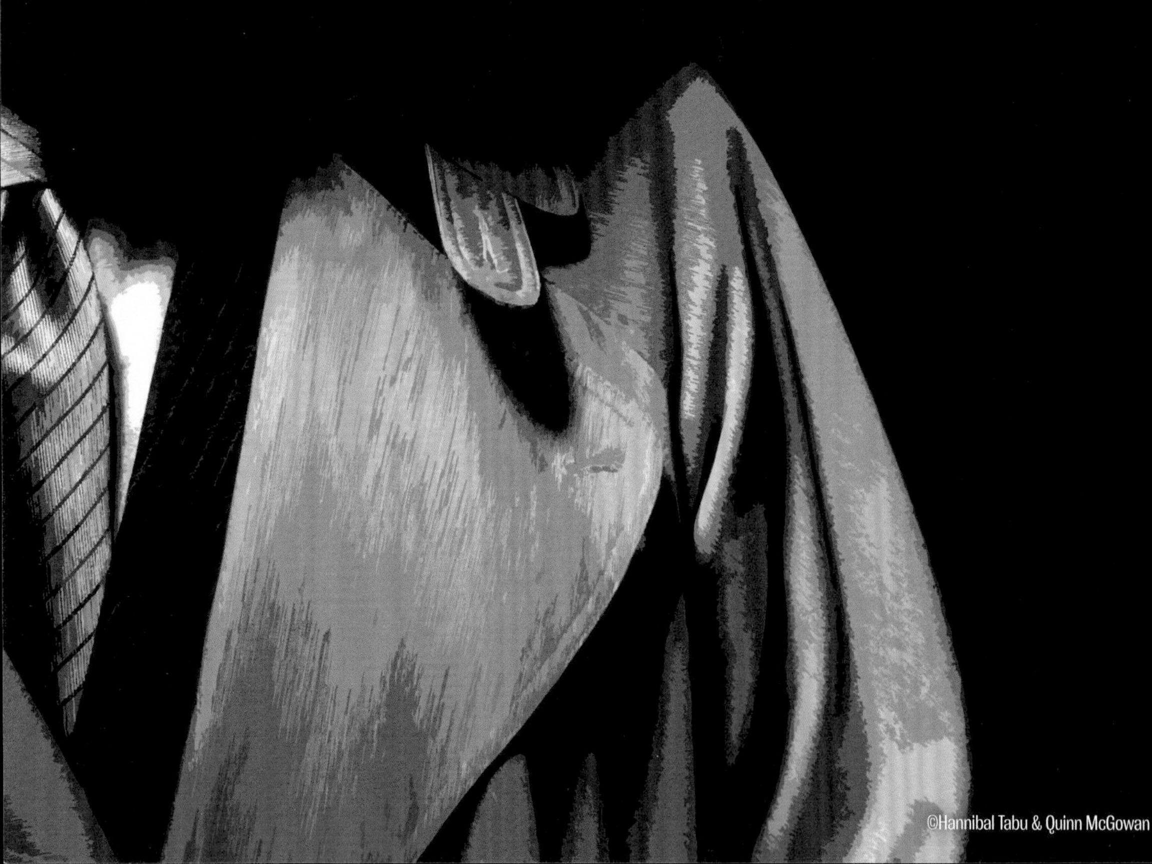

1:15 PM, MAY 19, RICKY'S WEST HOLLYWOOD.
RICKY'S
MY NAME IS NJAA WASHINGTON. THREE THINGS ABOUT ME...
I'M NON-BINARY AND ASEXUAL, WHICH CONFUSES LOTS OF PEOPLE.
I'VE TRAVELED THE WORLD, BUT ALWAYS ENDED UP BACK IN LOS ANGELES.
I HATE BARS.

STRAIGHT OR OTHERWISE, BARS ARE MEAT MARKETS. SO...UGH. TONIGHT, THERE IS SOMETHING I WANT: DAN RUCK.
HE'S ONE OF THE BIGGEST DONORS TO L.A.'S POWERS THAT BE, A STRUCTURE THAT'S BEEN THE SAME FOREVER. HE'S UNTOUCHABLE.
HE ALSO HAS A TASTE FOR YOUNG, BLACK GUYS. CREEPY OLD WHITE GUYS IN GAY BARS PICKING UP YOUNG GUYS OF COLOR: GROSS, BUT ACCEPTED.
HOWEVER...THREE TIMES THIS YEAR, YOUNG BLACK MEN WENT HOME WITH DAN RUCK...AND DIED THERE.

THE DISTRICT ATTORNEY IS OLD MONEY ON RUCK'S TEAT. THERE'S NO CHANCE HE'LL BE CHARGED. HE *LITERALLY* GOT AWAY WITH *MURDER.*
NO H8

NO H8
MY PARENTS RAISED ME TO KNOW ALL COPS ARE BAD. RUCK WILL NEVER PAY FOR WHAT HE DID...UNLESS SOMEONE *MAKES* HIM PAY.

I'M NOT TALKING ABOUT A CIVIL SUIT.
I HAVE *OTHER* IDEAS.

RUCK SPENDS HIS WAY INTO PEOPLE'S PANTS, GETS THEM HOME, DRUGS THEM UP... AND STUFF GOES WRONG.
NO H8
PEOPLE LIKE MY FRIEND D.K.

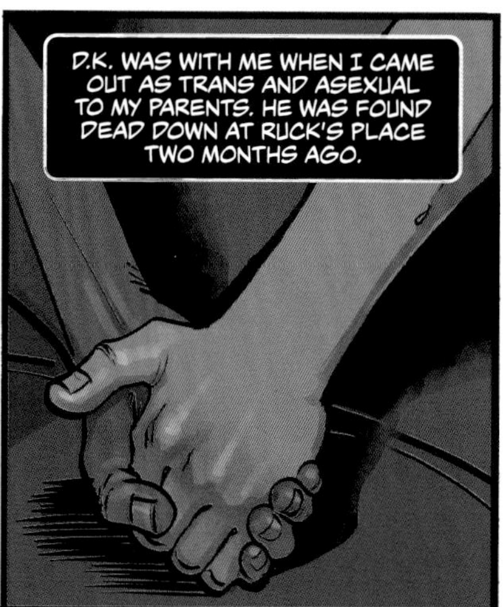
D.K. WAS WITH ME WHEN I CAME OUT AS TRANS AND ASEXUAL TO MY PARENTS. HE WAS FOUND DEAD DOWN AT RUCK'S PLACE TWO MONTHS AGO.

OUTSIDE OF RICKY'S, 1:12 AM
NO H8
THREE MONTHS BEFORE, GEMMY MOORE TURNED UP O.D.'D THERE TOO.

CASHMERE'S WITH HIM TONIGHT...

THINGS ARE *NOT* GONNA GO THE SAME WAY.

MY GREAT-GRANDMOTHER WAS IN THE BLACK PANTHER PARTY.
NOTICE
CENTURY PLAZA TOWERS, SOUTH SERVICE ENTRANCE. 1:27 AM.

CENTURY PLAZA TOWERS, NORTH TOWER LOBBY, 1:28 AM.

MY GRANDPARENTS MET AT BLACK LIVES MATTER PROTESTS IN THEIR TEENS.

MY PARENTS TAUGHT ME SURVIVALISM WHILE OTHER KIDS PLAYED ROBLOX AND FORTNITE.

I CAN'T LIVE FOR THE MOVEMENT LIKE MY FOLKS, BUT I CAN'T LET WRONG GO UNCHECKED.

NORMALLY THAT'S SOME HACKING HERE, A TAX AUDIT THERE.

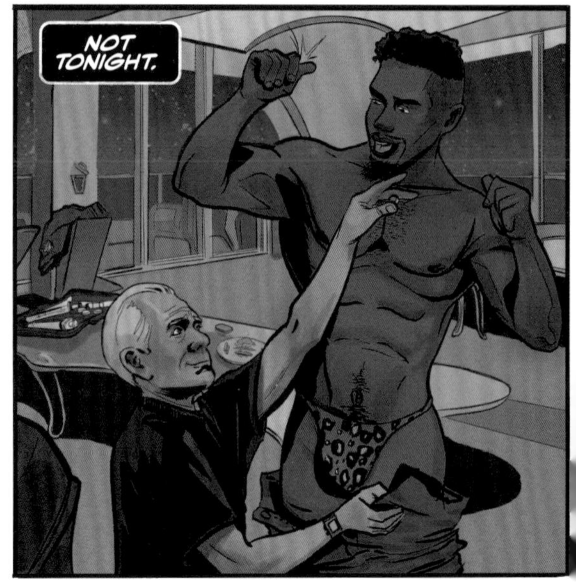
NOT TONIGHT.

ALMOST READY AND... WAIT, WHAT? I CAN'T BELIEVE THE NERVE OF THIS GUY...

HE STILL HAS DK'S JACKET?! MY MOTHER SAID VIOLENCE IS THE FIRST CHOICE OF THE UNWISE...

...BUT MY DAD SUGGESTED THAT WAS PRIVILEGE AND ACCESS TALKING.

SORRY, MAMA...
BOOOMMM

NO NO NO NO NO!
I'M TOO PRETTY FOR JAIL!!!

THERE'S A SAYING IN MY DAD'S FAMILY: 'IT AIN'T WRONG TILL THEY CATCH YOU.' MOM HATED THAT.

GOOD, HIS WATCH IS CLOSE ENOUGH TO HIS PHONE TO UNLOCK IT. PHONES ARE HARD TO HACK. WATCHES, NOT SO MUCH.

...BUYING HEROIN, LAWYER CONVERSATIONS, HUSH MONEY...AND ALL LEAKED TO EVERY PAPER OF RECORD IN THE COUNTRY.
RIGHT NOW.

THAT GOT ATTENTION. ALREADY TRENDING.
PING!
PING!
PING!
PING!
PING!
PING!

EVERYBODY KNOWS THE TRUTH NOW, RUCK. NOW...
WHO'S NEXT?
POLICE
END OF LINE.

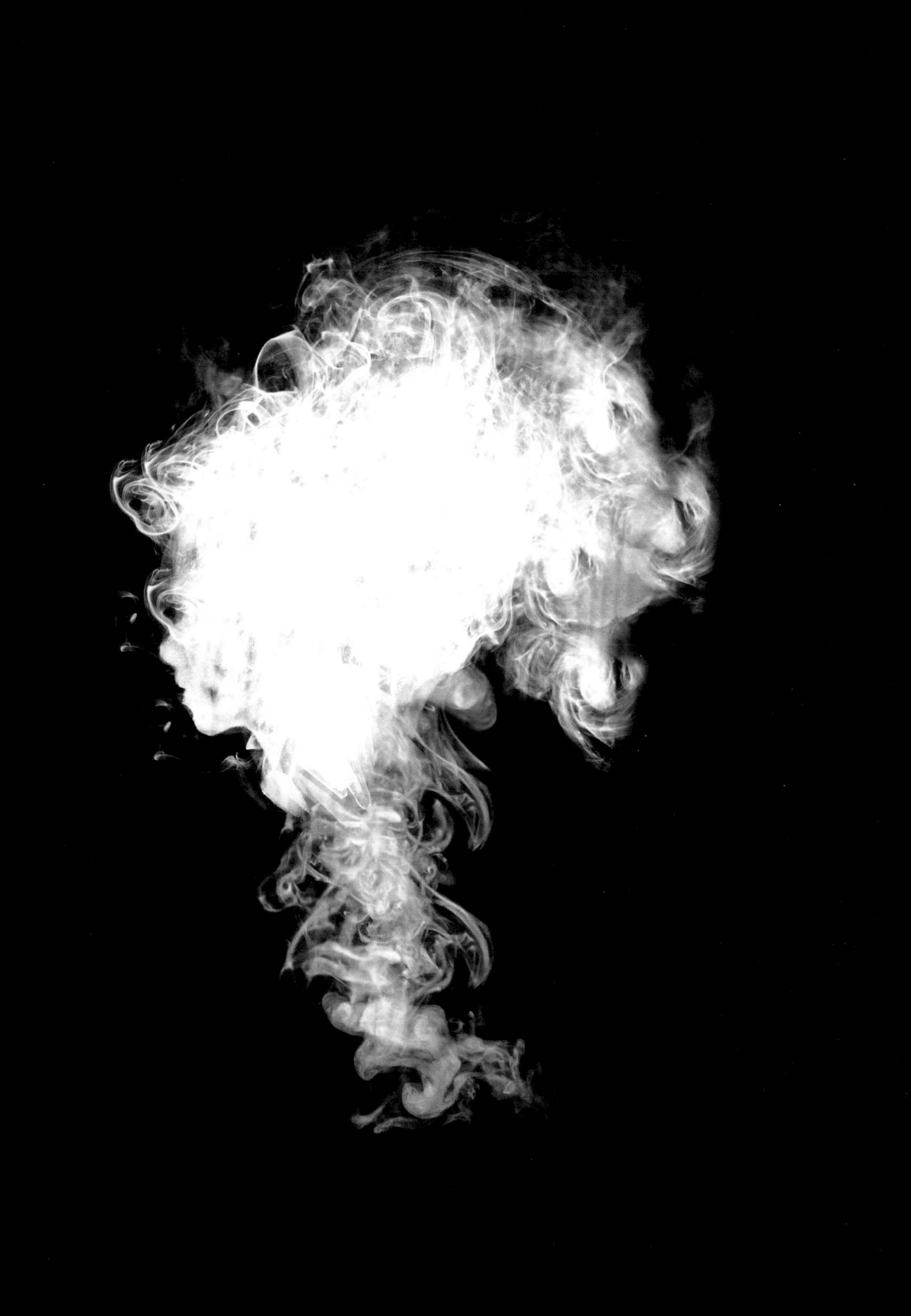

IGBO LANDING

STORY: MELODY COOPER ART: EDER MESSIAS

COLORS: PARIS ALLEYNE

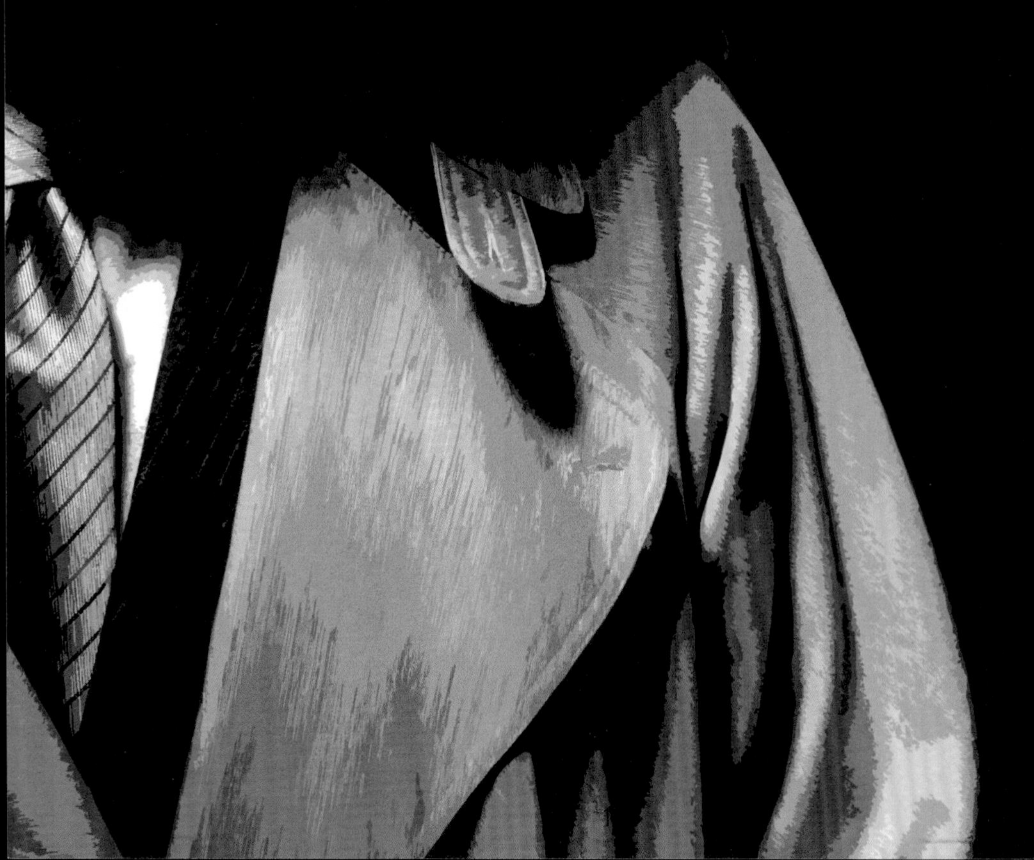

THAT'S HIM.

JAMAL, HOW IS HE AVOIDING THE BIO SENSORS?

SECURITY CAM CAUGHT HIM ON SECTOR FIVE'S WALL LAST WEEK.

THAT'S WHERE THE INFECTION STARTED.
THEN HE'S FROM INVIDIA. IT'S ANOTHER ATTACK.
WE NEED TO STOP HIM, BREE.

"...RIGHT NOW."
IGBO
LANDING

INVIDIA

WILL IT WORK?
WE ALMOST DESTROYED THEM ONCE. IT'S OUR LEGACY TO TRY.

THERE ARE 200 FAMILIES IN THIS SECTOR.
TAKE HIM.

DAMN!
THRAAACK

THE INTRUDER IS ABOUT TO BREACH THE OUTER PERIMETER.
STAND DOWN.
WHAT!?
WE HAVE NEW INFO. RETURN HOME.

THIS IS BULLSHIT.
WE APPRECIATE ALL YOU'VE DONE TO TRACK THESE INTRUDERS, BUT THERE'S BEEN A SHOCKING DEVELOPMENT.
LEON, IT BETTER BE THAT SOMEONE ELSE TOOK HIM OUT ON THE OTHER SIDE OF THE WALL.
DR. LEWIS, WHY DON'T YOU SHARE THE LATEST INFO?

IT LOOKS LIKE WE HAVEN'T HAD ANY DEATHS FROM THE INFECTION.

INFECTION? BIOLOGICAL WARFARE.
EVERYONE WHO'S HAD THE VIRUS HAS RECOVERED.
THAT DOESN'T MEAN INVIDIA GETS A PASS.

AFTER WHAT THEY DID TO OUR FIRST SHIP, AND THEN TO THE COLONY WHEN WE BUILT IT FASTER AND BETTER THAN THEIRS?
MY FATHER DIED PROTECTING IGBO LANDING.

THE VIRUS THEY ATTACKED US WITH HAS GIVEN US SOMETHING ELSE.

"THE RECOVERED ARE MORE POWERFUL..."

"THEIR UNDERLYING CONDITIONS HAVE BEEN HEALED."

PLEASE TELL ME YOU'RE NOT GOING TO SAY WHATEVER DOESN'T KILL US--
--- MAKES US STRONGER? IN THIS CASE, ABSOLUTELY YES.
WHATEVER THEY THOUGHT THIS WOULD DO TO US, IT HAS HAD UNINTENDED SIDE EFFECTS.

THEY'VE TRIED IT BEFORE. FROM ROSEWOOD AND TULSA TO SENECA VILLAGE AND WILMINGTON.
WHENEVER WE'RE SUCCESSFUL, THEY COME FOR US. IT DOESN'T MATTER WHAT PLANET WE'RE ON. THIS TIME, IT'S WORKED TO OUR--
WATCH OUT!
AAAARGH!
PEW

INVIDIA WHITE TRASH!

WHAT THE--

DAMN
LEON, HE'S ONE OF US.
NO. HE'S *NOT* ONE OF US. HIS SORRY TRAITOR ASS IS NOT AN IGBO LANDER.

YOU WEREN'T HAPPY WITH FOOD AND SHELTER?
CLEAN WATER? A PLACE TO CALL HOME WITH YOUR OWN?
THE HELL WITH YOU. THEY OFFERED ME MORE. A WHOLE SECTOR. AND REAL POWER.
WOW. THIS FOOL REALLY BELIEVES THEIR LIES.

SO YOU ENDANGERED OUR LIVES TO HELP THEM AND TO GET YOUR OWN PIECE OF NOTHING?
AAAIIIEE!!
JAMAL, NO. REMEMBER OUR OATH.
HE SHOULD NEVER FORGET: "LIFE IS SACRED."

SHE'S RIGHT. THERE'S A BETTER WAY TO DEAL WITH HIM.
JUST BY BEING HERE HE HAS GAINED SOMETHING THAT WE CAN SHARE WITH INVIDIA. LET A HIGHER POWER DECIDE THEIR FATE.

HEY, CAMERON. LOOKS LIKE THE NATIVE LIFE IS NOT TOO HAPPY TO SEE YOU.

YOU KNOW WHAT'S OUT THERE. YOU CAN'T LEAVE ME.
WE CAN DO WHATEVER THE HELL WE WANT.
YOU DECIDED WHO TO THROW IN WITH.
WE'RE JUST GONNA THROW YOU BACK.

SCREEEEEEEE
MMPHHH

"WHILE OUR COLONY RECOVERS, THERE'S INTEL THAT INVIDIA IS NOT SO LUCKY."

THE INFECTION THE INTRUDER TOOK BACK WITH HIM HAS SPREAD INCREDIBLY FAST.
BY THEIR OWN HAND, THEIR HATRED CHOKES THEIR OWN THROAT.
THEY NEVER LEARN.
THE ANCESTORS HAVE A SAYING: "HE WHO HOLDS ME TO THE GROUND HOLDS HIMSELF."
TRUER WORDS...
...WERE NEVER SPOKEN.
THE END.

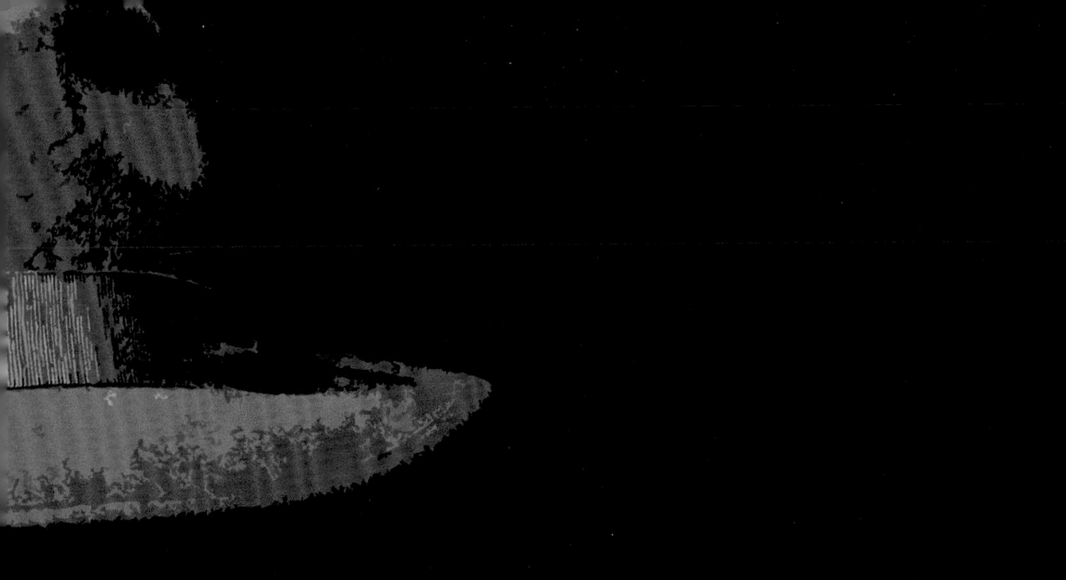

C.A.N.O.P.Y

STORY: BRANDON THOMAS
ART: N.STEVEN HARRIS
COLORS: WALT BARNA

BAR
CLOSING TIME @ KADEEJA'S BAR

ZZZ... ZZZZZ... ZZZ...
MS. JAMES...? MS. JAMES, I'M CLOSING UP NOW...
SNNKK MHM?
HOW-- HOW LONG'S IT BEEN, DEE?
NOT LONG AT ALL.
IT'S JUST YOU AND WHOEVER THAT GUY IS OVER THERE. YOU NEED A CAB?
NAH, IT'S NICE OUT.

SORRY FOR THE TROUBLE.
NO TROUBLE MAN...ALL STAY WELCOME.
THANKS, DEE, I'LL DO BETTER NEXT TIME.
RYA, I'VE TOLD YOU TO STOP ALL THAT.
"WHATEVER YOU NEED" MEANS EXACTLY THAT.
MARS... IN THE FUTURE
THANK YOU FOR YOUR SERVICE!
YOU ARE VERY WELCOME, PRETTY GIRL...

LOOK AT YOU, LOOK AT YOU--END OF THE NIGHT, AND YOU STILL ALIVE...

GOOD FOR YOU, RYA JAMES.

ZZZ--
SNKKK--
ZZZZ--
KNOCK
KNOCK
KNOCK
COME ON NOW, IT'S *SUPPOSED* TO BE SATURDAY...
RYA JAMES...?
COMMANDER JAMES?
HEY.
YEAH.
IT'S JUST REGULAR RYA NOW.
OKAY.
SOMEONE'S DEAD, AND THEY TOLD ME YOU COULD HELP, SO--I DON'T KNOW--***COME HELP.***

RISER 5
ASSIGNED PILOT:
NASIR UNDERWOOD
SO MUCH DAMN SPACE IN HERE NOW.
YOU SHOULD'VE *SEEN* THESE THINGS BACK IN MY DAY. COULD BARELY EVEN BREATHE.
YES, EXACTLY, *LET'S TALK ABOUT THAT.*
LET'S HAVE A LITTLE LESS ATTITUDE, AND A LITTLE MORE EXPLANATORY DIALOGUE, YOUNG MAN.
AIN'T *NOBODY* OLD ENOUGH TO AVOID AN ASS-WHOOPING.
THERE'S BEEN A MURDER--ONE OF THE OLDER EX-PILOTS... LIKE YOU...

WELL... I GUESS I SHOULD SAY THERE'S BEEN ANOTHER MURDER.
IN THE PAST COUPLE MONTHS, THERE HAVE BEEN THREE FORMER PILOTS OR COMMANDERS FOUND UNDER SUSPICIOUS CIRCUMSTANCES. INITIALLY, THEY SUSPECTED SUICIDE, WHICH IS COMMON AMONG YOU FIRST AND SECOND WAVERS, BUT--
AFTER MAL MARRIS WAS FOUND DEAD...? WELL, THAT CHANGED EVERYTHING.
NO WAY HE TAKES HIMSELF OUT. NO WAY.
"POOR GUY WAS FOUND IN HIS HOME TOTALLY ALONE.
"HE MISSED WORK ONE MORNING, AND SOMEONE CALLED IN AN INTEGRITY CHECK.
"HAD TO SMASH HIS DOOR DOWN AND EVERYTHING.
"NOBODY HAD EVEN SEEN HIM THE NIGHT BEFORE--
"BUT HE'D TURNED INTO A REAL LONER SINCE HE AGED OUT.
"GUESS IT WAS ALL THAT TRAUMA, YOU KNOW?
"STILL, AFTER ALL HE ACCOMPLISHED-- THE LIVES HE PERSONALLY SAVED?
"HE DESERVED BETTER THAN BEING SHOT TO DEATH WITH NO WARNING.
COMMAND THOUGHT WE SHOULD START AT THE CRIME SCENE.
THAT SOUNDS LIKE THEM. ONE TINY THING THOUGH...

I SEE YOUR MAN BACK THERE, JUST LIKE I SAW HIM BACK IN DEE'S BAR.
SEE, I CAN PRETEND I'M DRUNK TOO, BUT HE DIDN'T TAKE THE BAIT THEN, LEAVING YA'LL TO PLAN THIS OTHER NONSENSE INSTEAD.

IF IT WAS UP TO ME... I'D JUST KILL YOU BOTH, MAIL THE HEADS BACK TO YOUR MASTERS ON EARTH WITH A QUICK NOTE TO FUCK THE FUCK OFF. BUT I'M TRYING TO BE--BETTER IN MY OLD AGE.
RISER 5, EXECUTIVE OVERRIDE CODE 11617--THIS IS RYA JAMES CALLING IN A NEURAL SPIKE. NOW WOULD BE GOOD, THANKS.

HELLO, RYA. IT HAS BEEN A WHILE.
YEAH, SORRY FOR THE TROUBLE.
NO TROUBLE AT ALL. THEY WILL REMAIN CONSCIOUS FOR ANOTHER FEW SECONDS. I FEEL LIKE YOU'RE ANXIOUS TO SAY SOMETHING ELSE.

YOU BOYS JUST GOT HIT WITH A NEURAL SPIKE THAT--FUNNY STORY, DOESN'T EFFECT NORMAL HUMANS.
YOUR SISTERS TRIED SOMETHING SIMILAR TO THIS WAY BACK WHEN, SO WE BOOBYTRAPPED ALL THE COCKPITS.
GET ME CENTRAL COMMAND, RISER 5.

YEAH, BOTH TARGETS ARE DOWN, AND READY FOR INTERROGATION. YOU WERE RIGHT, THEY COULDN'T RESIST MAKING A RUN AT ME TOO.
YOU KNOW HOW I FEEL ABOUT IT, BUT--WE NEED TO RECOMMISSION THE WOLVES PROTECTORATE.
RIGHT NOW.
Only the beginning...

PINUP BY **MAKENA**

NO OUTLET

STORY: GARY PHILLIPS ART: DAVID BRAME
COLORS: PARIS ALLEYNE

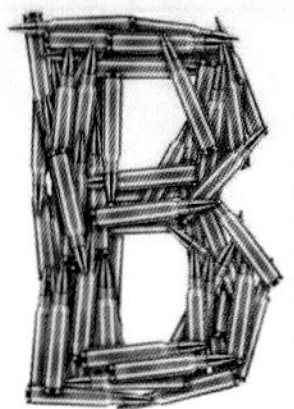

utler gripped the M.D. by the upper arm. He was aided by Kramer, a cold-eyed short-haired blonde aiming her AR 15 at their captive's spine.
"You can't get away with this," the woman said, her hands zip tied in front of her as they hustled her through the doorway.
"We already have, doc," Butler huffed.

Kramer slung her rifle across her back and replaced the stout plank in the brackets they'd screwed in place to barricade the front door. There were elephant high hedges boarding the house that long since needed taming. The yard between those hedges and the house were overgrown with weeds, foxtails and dumped trash. Plywood had been hammered in place over glassless windows. Some of these boards had been taken down and dirty sheets had been tacked up in their place over time All this helped blocked a view of the five of them coming and going from the once habitable abode. Mostly though at this point they kept inside, except for this daring kidnapping Butler had concocted. There was graffiti on the walls, and it was evident the abandoned house had been used by squatters and as a shooting gallery by drug users. Broken discarded plastic hypodermics were everywhere underfoot.

Battery powered lanterns for light had been placed in various areas of the house. What had been the backyard was more overgrown than the front.
Butler escorted the physician through the once living room. There were three others in there, similarly garbed and armed. The quintet were members of a self-styled citizens' militia called the Broken Snake. Their name inspired by the image of the coiled rattler on the 'Don't Tread on Me' flag of the Continental Marines. The idea being the trans loving liberals had broken the promise of the United States and it was their duty to restore the American Way as God intended.
"Oh, Christ," Dr. Deidra "Dee" Blanchard said, shaking her head. *"You can't possibly expect me to operate in these conditions."*
Butler pointed at the man who'd been placed on one of the plywood boards laid atop one of the few pieces of intact furniture, the kitchen table. *"That's my big brother laying there, doctor. I expect you to do everything you can to save his life. Or we take you and yours, it's just that simple."*
Strapped to the outside of his lower pant leg, Butler removed a sheathed Bowie knife. He used this to cut Blanchard's restraint. His big brother groaned and writhed some where he lay on his back, his legs at the knees draped over the edge.
His body armor and shirt had been stripped off, the bandaging on his lower side was seeped crimson.
She bit back a sarcastic comment about encouraging them to go after her skirt chasing ex-husband. *"Let me explain what's simple. Rubbing alcohol, tweezers, rubber gloves and this other stuff you lifted from a CVS isn't going to be sufficient. If you intend to shoot me anyway, then you should do it now."*
Kramer eyed her balefully.
When they'd stuck the muzzle of a gun in her ribs as she walked to work, Blanchard had determined then that trying to placate these alt-white assholes was a waste of time. They knew she was a doctor because she'd been taped by the news in front of her hospital voicing support for the protestors. She wouldn't intentionally try to antagonize these fools, but she'd be damned if she was going to play the terrified prisoner. Particularly being black, she wasn't going to give them the satisfaction.
Butler frowned at her.
Kramer, standing in the doorway, said, "You mean you need proper shit from the hospital."
"That's right."
The gathered were well aware that out on the streets riot-jacked police riding bold in their military-issued MRAPs, Mine Resistant Ambush Protected Vehicles with their mounted sound canons were prowling the boulevards for straggler protestors in this early morning hour. Anxious to make a few ear drums of brown rice eater bleed.
"Can't be done," Butler said.
Blanchard stepped close to the wounded man. She ripped away the bloody gauze and cotton squares on the wound, the dressing already loose.
"Hey," Butler said, jamming the muzzle of her pistol against her temple.
Slowly and calmly the doctor said, "Have the bullets fragmented inside of him? Is a piece in his stomach now, has another piece punctured his duodenum, his small intestine?"
"Can't you find that out?" Butler said, lowering his weapon and worrying his bottom lip.
"Sure, cutting him open and using a probe will tell me a lot. You all figure this is the wild west anyway. I'm supposed to use that pig-sticker of yours to slice into him?"
"Motherfucker," he said to no one in particular. He looked at Kramer.
"She's got to be able to anesthetize him," Kramer said, lifting a shoulder. *"The longer we wait, the more chance sepsis or some other damn problem sets in. Then we rip off the hospital,"* Butler said.
Blanchard said nothing.

"We need her to get us inside," Kramer pointed out as one of the others wrapped the wound again. *"Of course though security is going to be on alert at any hospital."*

Butler looked from her to the doctor and said, *"I guess you're right."*

"This is bullshit," another member of the group said from behind Kramer. He was called Little Feet for his size fifteen boots.

"How do you plan to pull that off, Bryce? Huh? Gonna waltz into the hospital in your fatigues and what not?" They had worn their battle gear when they'd arrived in town to protest the anti-police protesters.

"There's no choice, man," Butler growled. *"That's one of our soldiers lying there. He's wounded because he stood up for our principals. You'd want us to expend all possible effort if it was you on the table."*

"I'd also want my crew to know when it was advisable to take another course."

"It's not time to cut and run, Little Feet."

"Is that so?"

"Yeah, it is."

"We can do this," Kramer said. *"We have to."*

They were now standing in the front room. Blanchard rubbed her wrists to aid in circulation. Idly, though she jogged regularly, she knew she had no chance to make a run for it. Each one of them either had an assault rifle or at least a semi-auto holstered on their hip. She'd worked ER too long to not appreciate the direct and

collateral damage one bullet could do the human body let alone several tearing through flesh, bone and organs.
One of them said, *"Then it's you two going in, we secure the perimeter."*
Blanchard kept her face neutral. Inside her hospital would be her best chance to get one up on these bastards.
"Just me and Kramer on this," Butler announced. *"Kramer as a woman has a better chance going in with the doc, pretending to be wounded than if I came along. Besides, I'll be the one securing the perimeter. If they don't come back in the required time, then poof goes whoever I find at the doc's house."* They'd taken her backpack and gone though her wallet she had in it, noting her address on her driver's license.
"You understand what I'm saying, Blanchard?"
"I do. Though I am curious why you chose me for this glorious task."
"You kidding, you're famous," Kramer sneered. "Plus what delicious irony, right?"
"Yeah" Blanchard said dryly.
At the door Butler said to the remaining three. *"If we don't make it back, you go to the doc's house and take care of anybody you find there. Understand?"*

Putting together from what she'd read on the newsfeed on her phone earlier yesterday, Blanchard surmised Butler's brother must have been the unidentified armed man who'd been in a shootout with two officers on foot patrol. This was right before matters ratcheted up as night descended. The brother had been exiting a discount convenience store, cash trailing in the wind from the plastic shopping bag he was carrying. It was surmised from the grainy store video and the clerk who'd been beaten that the robbery had been a spur of the moment sort of thing. The armed man had entered the store berating the turbaned Sikh proprietor, calling him all sorts of derogatory names, get out of America and on and on.
The cops spotted the brother from across the street and told him to halt as they drew their sidearms. The brother had his assault rifle strapped on him in such a way that he was able to bring it level and fire. He did and the police returned fire. The SUV the group had come to town in roared into view from around a near corner, those inside laying down cover fire. The vehicle slowed to a roll just long enough for them to yank their wounded member inside, and blazed away. Because of the wounded man, they took the risk of getting to the empty house in the SUV, which was traveling in town on stolen license plates. Occupying the house wasn't by happenstance.

"Yes," Little Feet said.
Blanchard was taking care of her mother who was undergoing cancer treatments. She willed her knees not to buckle as she walked toward the door, Kramer beside her.
The three exited the house and went along the walkway, what was visible of it. There was little gap now between the bordering hedges where the walkway ended. In years past, when the hedges, over seven feet high, had been maintained, they served as a green barrier between the yard and the sidewalk. These days they were wild tangled growth the three stepped through onto an empty thoroughfare as if emerging from a forest primeval into civilization.
"Keep steppin'," Butler said.
They were heading toward the car they'd brought her here in, parked two blocks away. This was not the vehicle they driven to town. But one they'd snatched from a shopper returning to their car at a grocery store. Sure the car was reported stolen, but the owner had been attacked from behind and hadn't gotten a look at his attackers who'd gun-butted him to the ground, dazing him. While the cops were searching for the brother, they hadn't at this time tied the two incidents together.

The big march and rally protesting the latest suspect killing of an unarmed black man by the police had occurred 10 days ago. Once again the act had been captured on a ubiquitous camera phone, two in fact. Outraged, yet again, several mainstream and left groups had planned the mass action for yesterday, a Saturday. So had the response of the Broken Snakes. But unlike some of their compatriots who would simply arrive on this day hoisting tiki torches with Confederate flags waving from them to antagonize the muff diving diversifiers, Kramer had been sent to town several days ago to do advance scouting. She'd worn civilian garb for her undercover mission. What with her don't' fuck-with-me attitude and tatts, she fit right in with the tree hugging SJWs she'd noted with disdain.
Leaving the epicenter of the protest and counter-protest was easier than going back toward it, even now at this supposed quiet hour. Here and there as they drove along, dark agglomerations of people moving as if of one body walked in the roadways. Grey smoke lit from below could be seen by those in the car in the near distance as they got closer to the downtown area. They drive past an overturned, charred hulk of a car and torched stores.

"Easy now," Kramer said from the back seat where she sat next to Blanchard guarding her as Butler drove. A bonfire burned in the middle of the road, the double yellow lines leading right to it as if by design.

"Hey, that's one of them," someone shouted as the car went past the fire, the flame illuminating Butler at the wheel.

"Shit," he swore, depressing the accelerator.

A Molotov cocktail was tossed, bursting against the windshield. Flaming gas spread across the now spider-webbed glass and the hood.

"Goddammit," Butler swore, swerving as rocks and bottles were also thrown against the car as a contingent of semi-lit shapes chased the car. The gas on the hood still burned but soon went out. A black man with dreads flailing like sentient tendrils from a red, white and blue handkerchief leaped onto the trunk. He was splayed there somehow hanging on with one hand with a brick in the other, intending to bust out the back window. But upon seeing Blanchard, he momentarily hesitated, unsure as to why this black woman was in this car with these two white rightists.

Kramer freed her pistol to shoot the man and Blanchard knocked her arm aside, the shot going through the roof. The startled man let go and rolled across the asphalt.

"Bitch," Kramer said, jabbing Blanchard hard in the gut with the gun, making her grunt and grimace.

"We need her alive," Butler advised drolly as they drove on.

"Yeah, yeah," Kramer said.

They proceeded unmolested for several miles. But nearing the downtown area, they could see there was a roadblock ahead, less than two blocks away. MRAPs were turned sideways in the street and police were out in force controlling egress only. Several protestors milled about too.

"I'm sure it's like that no matter which way we want to get in." Kramer had been trying to view a newsfeed on her phone. But as there was no signal though should have been here in the heart of the city in the canyon of all these highrises. She concluded the law was jamming the signal.

"Then we go in on foot." Butler pulled to the curb, a no parking zone, and killed the engine. Getting transportation back wasn't a concern. The three got out, moving into the deeper gloom of a building's alcove so as not to be as visible. Butler and Kramer flanked the

doctor in their camo gear and body armor.
"We better do something to better blend in," Kramer said, aware of how they contrasted Blanchard's attire of jeans, a buttoned-up shirt and light pullover sweater. Both had left their long guns at the house but both had sidearms. Butler of course had brought his knife along as well.
"Okay," Butler agreed, unbuckling his armor from his torso.
Kramer took hers off too and they put these in the trunk of the car. A woman wearing the cosplay costume of Captain Marvel, a top hat with a large swirl patterned circle attached to its crown rolled by on a bicycle. She stared at them and they her. She rode on, away from downtown.
"Needless to say, as much as possible, we stick to the side streets," Butler announced as the three marched toward downtown. A purple light hazed the horizon, daybreak approaching. Between them and the barricade was a rise in the roadway. Underneath this were freeway lanes, the traffic perpendicular to the above. There was a narrow series of stairs next to the overpass and the three took to these, descending as they did so to a street below. Coming up the stairs were two others, a man and woman. She was of olive-complexion, and he appeared to be mixed race, of black and white

parentage. The woman had on a black bandanna wrapped around her lower face. Blanchard tensed and Kramer pressed against the doctor hissing in her ear. *"Say anything and their blood is on your hands."*
"What's with the get-up?" The man and woman had stopped, blocking the way. He shook a finger at Butler and Kramer. *"I've seen this kind of outfit, haven't you?"* he said to his companion.
"Yeah," she drawled, zeroing her gaze on Butler. *"Like them flag wavers for Jesus,"* she chuckled.
"Make America white again," the man said, bristling.
"But what are you doing with them, sister?"
"They're my friends," Blanchard said. *"They dressed this way to blend in."*
"Spies, huh?" the woman said, her dubious tone evident.
Butler and Kramer had pulled their shirt tails out, the guns tucked in their waistbands underneath. The Broken Snakes leader's hand hovered over that area. *"Everything's cool, man."*
"Really?" the other one said.
"Yes, please," Blanchard said, *"we need to be on our way."*
"Time is tight is it?" the masked woman said.
Blanchard put a hand on her arm.
"You don't know how tight." She squeezed gently then withdrew her hand.
They stood staring at one another for several beats. Finally the two who'd been coming up the stairs stood to one side to let the other three pass. The two men though couldn't help but glare at one another, waiting for the other one to flex. On the street below the three picked up the pace.
Down passageways between buildings, cutting through a pocket park where a homeless man slept in his makeshift tent and clambering up over a wall they had to jump up to grab the top of, the three kept mostly away from patrols or other pedestrians, no matter why they might be out at this early hour. But as they jaywalked a wide thoroughfare less than four blocks from Commonwealth Memorial, a siren blurped at them from up the block.
"Fuck," Butler muttered. He moved a few steps away from the other two to get an unobstructed shot if need be.

Blanchard and Kramer stood close as if twins conjoined at the hip. The police car rolled toward them, their spotlight highlighting them even though the sun was rising.
"Where you all going?" said a policewoman from the car over her loudspeaker. She sat next to a male in the driver's seat.
"I'm a doctor," Blanchard announced. She held her hospital ID aloft. *"We're heading to Commonwealth,"* she called out. Under her breath but looking straight ahead she said, "If you don't let me talk to them, we all die right here and right now. That includes your brother, Butler."
"Go," he said. He and Kramer watched while Blanchard, holding her hands and ID up, walked over to the patrol car which had halted. Both officers were out of the car, the man with his hand on the butt of his holstered semi-auto.
"She could give us up," Kramer said.
"Well, she's black and they're both white. Yeah, she's a doc and we're dressed like this but still," he grinned. *"Look at Kenosha and homeboy strolling by the cops brandishing his weapon after popping caps in those Antifa lovers."*
Kramer looked at him then back at the cops. The female officer pointed toward her and Butler talking to Blanchard. Kramer noted Blanchard's relaxed body language as she responded to her question. At one point the doctor had her back turned to them, the two cops looking past her at the two as well. Minutes like drying paint went by. The female cop laughed at another point, nodding

her head. Eventually Blanchard started back toward them, the cops getting back in their car.

"What did you say to them?" Butler demanded.

"I charmed the fuck out of them," she hurled back. *"Let's get this over with."* Blanchard marched away toward their destination. Actually it turned out the woman officer recognized the doctor as she'd been inside Commonwealth Memorial several times lately, as she was dating a leggy nurse there. This familiarity helped smooth matters over, even though the male cop had seen her on TV and was icy toward her. Blanchard improvised on the spot, trying not to trip herself up. She told the officers a variation on what she'd told the progressive man and masked woman. Making sure to sound indignant as if she'd have anything to do with a couple of actual white rightists.

Kramer and Butler fell in step. Soon a block away, the hospital loomed before the three. Personnel came and went, some in scrubs and lab coats. Several said hello or nodded at Blanchard and she in turn acknowledged them. Butler's phone buzzed. Given the hospital's necessity, the signal wasn't jammed here.

As he listened, he stopped walking and his face became ashen.

"My brother's dead. They'd been trying to reach me for the last twenty minutes."

To Blanchard, Kramer said, *"Don't you have anything to say?"*

"Would it make a difference?"

When Blanchard had briefly examined the brother, she'd estimated he was two hours past when he should have been on an operating table. She was concerned his distended stomach might have indicated a bowel blockage due to the bullets fragmenting and it seemed her cursory diagnosis was correct. She hadn't of course mentioned her suspicion but frankly she didn't feel she'd betrayed her hypocritic oath. If it had been normal circumstances, she would have remained mum until confirmation.

"You're a dead woman," Butler announced, his voice flat with finality. *"Then your family."*

"Doc Dee, how's it going?"

The three turned to see an EMT walking by holding a Venti-sized capped cup of coffee and a breakfast burrito wrapped in tin foil.

"Hey, Brad." Blanchard lurched forward, clapping a hand on the man's shoulder.

"Ah, good to see you too."

Butler reached for the doctor and spun her around. As he did, she splashed the hot coffee she'd grabbed from the EMT in his face.

"Motherfuckin' nigger," he yelled, steam rising from his burned face.

"I got you, nigger, bitch." She kicked him in the nuts.

Kramer reached for her gun. Blanchard rammed her heel into the other woman's instep as she'd been taught in her self-defense classes. You didn't last long in ER dealing with all sorts of irate gang members or meth-addled significant others if you didn't know how to handle yourself. She got her in a hold and flipped her onto her back, intending to twist her arm and hopefully dislocate her shoulder.

Brad, also having contended with various types of obstreperous individuals in his career as an emergency tech had seen Butler going for his gun too. He freed the mini-canister of pepper spray clipped to his belt and blasted the stuff into the eyes of the leader of the Broken Snakes. Butler had the gun out and started firing, but wasn't able to hit his intended targets given his blurred vision. Blanchard and Brad tackled him and got him down to the ground. By this time security had been alerted and four burly men and a svelte woman came running. As they clubbed the shit out of Butler, Blanchard could see that Kramer had slipped away.

"Mama," she uttered, her nose bloody from being punched by Butler

"What the hell's going on her, Doc?" Brad asked.

"Gimme the keys to your RA."

"What?"

"Please, now."

"Sure."

Kramer approached a car stopped at a red light. The sun was up and early morning commuters where heading to work. She tapped the working end of her gun against the driver's side glass. The man looked over and his mouth gaped open, pieces of his egg biscuit sandwich falling from his lips onto his crisp starched dress shirt. She opened the unlocked door and he got out and wordlessly she got in and drove away. Kramer was keenly aware more than one onlooker on the sidewalk was videoing the incident with their phone cameras. She didn't give a fuck. This was a suicide mission anyway. She was comforted in her belief that Blanchard would not take the time to get a hold of the cops and try to explain what was going on. She knew whoever Kramer found at her home would be cooling on the hardwood floor by then. She also knew Blanchard would probably have a home with those kind of floors and wainscoting as well.

She imagined they'd both grown up in similar circumstances, a single parent mom always struggling to keep the rug rats fed, one shitty boyfriend after the next. But affirmative action, race traitors and Professional Negro Naysayers had given her more than a boost up. She gotten the goddamn keys. But where was her opportunity as a white person in the country her people helped build and defend?

"Shit," she swore, blowing through a stop light. Yes, the doctor was going to come at her and she was looking forward to their showdown.

Blanchard used the ambulance's siren to clear her way to her house. It seemed like forever but in less than twenty minutes, averaging 75 miles an hour according to the speedometer, she'd reached her neighborhood. She screeched around a corner, roaring past the No Outlet sign fronting the several linked streets all curving into each other. Blanchard drove along her street, eyeballing the surroundings for anything untoward. She parked behind her car in the driveway, the ambulance blocking the sidewalk, its boxy rear slopping into the street. She generally took the light rail into downtown.

Blanchard got out and tore inside. She carried a heavy pry bar kept in the ambulance. The tool was used to gain entry when a door was locked and the person on the other side was incapacitated. She was afraid to call out and more afraid on what might be waiting for her down the hallway to the bedrooms. That fear was the same reason she hadn't called her mother, assuming she could have been roused. Down the hall she went, feeling like an intruder in her own home. The door to her mother's room was ajar and her heart caught in the back of her throat.

Inexorably she went forward and eased the door further open. Her mother was in bed under a blanket. Conscious of her looks as far back as the daughter could remember, the former bartender had a handkerchief tied around her head even though she only had stubble for hair these days. The radio was on, low volume. It was the R&B oldies station she fell asleep to each early morning. Her mom Sadie usually wake around 2 a.m., then not be able to get back to sleep until 4 a.m. or so.

The current paperback novel she was reading was open face down on the nightstand. Blanchard stared hard in the half light, trying mightily to discern if the older woman was breathing. She got closer, using her surgeon's touch to put two fingers to the big vein in her neck. Her pulse was steady, at rest. Blanchard back-walked away and shut the door quietly. Back in her front room, shadowy still in the early light, she stood at the bow front windows overlooking the bucolic tree-lined street. A fatigue descended on her and she sat on an ottoman, the pry bar at her feet. It was as if the last hours were a bad dream she was only now waking from.

Engine revving, the car jumped the curb and went onto and sped across the tended lawn, creating twin earthen rivulets as it plowed through the front of the home, rattling the structure. Wood, glass, flagstone and sheetrock were blown aside. Blanchard was up but Kramer was already out of the driver's door shooting at her. Blanchard went down. The Broken Snake member clambered over the wreck of the front of the car, its ruined radiator leaking coolant and steam rising from it. Her boots crunched broken glass torn wood.

She approached the body of the doctor, smiling, anticipating enjoying her kill for a few seconds then fleeing the scene.

"The fuck?" she started, looking down.

"What's happening here?"

Kramer looked at the older black woman standing at the head of the hallway in the housecoat and rag askew around her head. She grinned, bringing her gun up.

Blanchard twisted around on the floor, striking Kramer in the lower leg with the pry bar as she took her shot. It missed her mother by inches.

"Mom, get in your room."

"Baby..."

"Mom," she pleaded.

Blanchard was on a knee as her mother shambled away. She sunk the end of the tool in Kramer's stomach as hard as she could, doubling her over.

On her feet, she brought the pry bar down on the other woman's wrist, eliciting a satisfying crack of bone. The gun dropped from her hand to the rug. Not knowing if she'd reach her house before Kramer, the ER seasoned Blanchard nonetheless had presence of mind and had made a stop on the way here. Using the pry bar, she popped opened the trunk of the discarded car and put on Kramer's body armor, tailored for a woman's form.

Kramer bowled into Blanchard's lower legs and the two combatants got tangled, grappling and punching at each other. Kramer slipped a rabbit punch on Blanchard's ribs and she buckled some. Sirens got closer. Kramer ran out the front door which was still intact in its frame. She got as far as the side of the crashed car and Blanchard brought her down from behind.

"Get off me," a desperate Kramer yelled, chewing dew wet grass as she was face down on the lawn. The automatic sprinklers had activated and began watering the lawn and the occupants.

The first police car on the scene had received the call from the dispatcher. Later it would be determined there had been a glitch in the communication from the neighbor calling in the disturbance at the doctor's house. Of the two officers who alighted from the vehicle, the one in the lead assumed the white woman was the doctor. Particularly as there was a black woman straddling her about to cave in her skull with a crowbar.

"Police," he yelled, *"drop the weapon,"* he added. Then in a blink of an eye he fired seven times and the aggressor went down. It would also later be determined that one of his rounds entered the eye of the blonde woman's head as she looked up. The bullet lodged in her brain.

One of his other rounds had struck Doctor Blanchard in the neck but had exited, without severing a major vein. She had though been knocked over and the same officer put a knee in her chest. Blanchard's windpipe had been affected and she couldn't talk.

"Don't you fuckin' move," the cop yelled at her. He was aiming his gun at her face as his partner kept the neighbors back.

Fortunately an older white woman named Agnes Burns who was friends with Blanchard and her mother said, *"What are you doing to Dr. Blanchard? Get off of her, now."*

Both officers looked at her and the black woman coughing up blood and bleeding into the lawn underneath the knee.

In the darkened room at Commonwealth Memorial, the door opened silently. Slanted light played across the inert form in the bed, monitors beeping and humming quietly. The old-fashioned clock above the bed read: 1:17 this a.m. Dee Blanchard stood at the bedside of the comatose Ellen Kramer. No one saw her enter. She'd studied the patient's charts and congruent with cases like this, it was anyone's guess as to if and when she might rouse from this state. And even then, given the path of the bullet, it seemed likely there would be some amount of brain damage.

But still, Blanchard weighed, there were numerous documented cases where the subject was able to function as before with the proper therapy. She reached out to one of the main wires with her gloved hand, grasping it, hesitating to disconnect the machine.

###

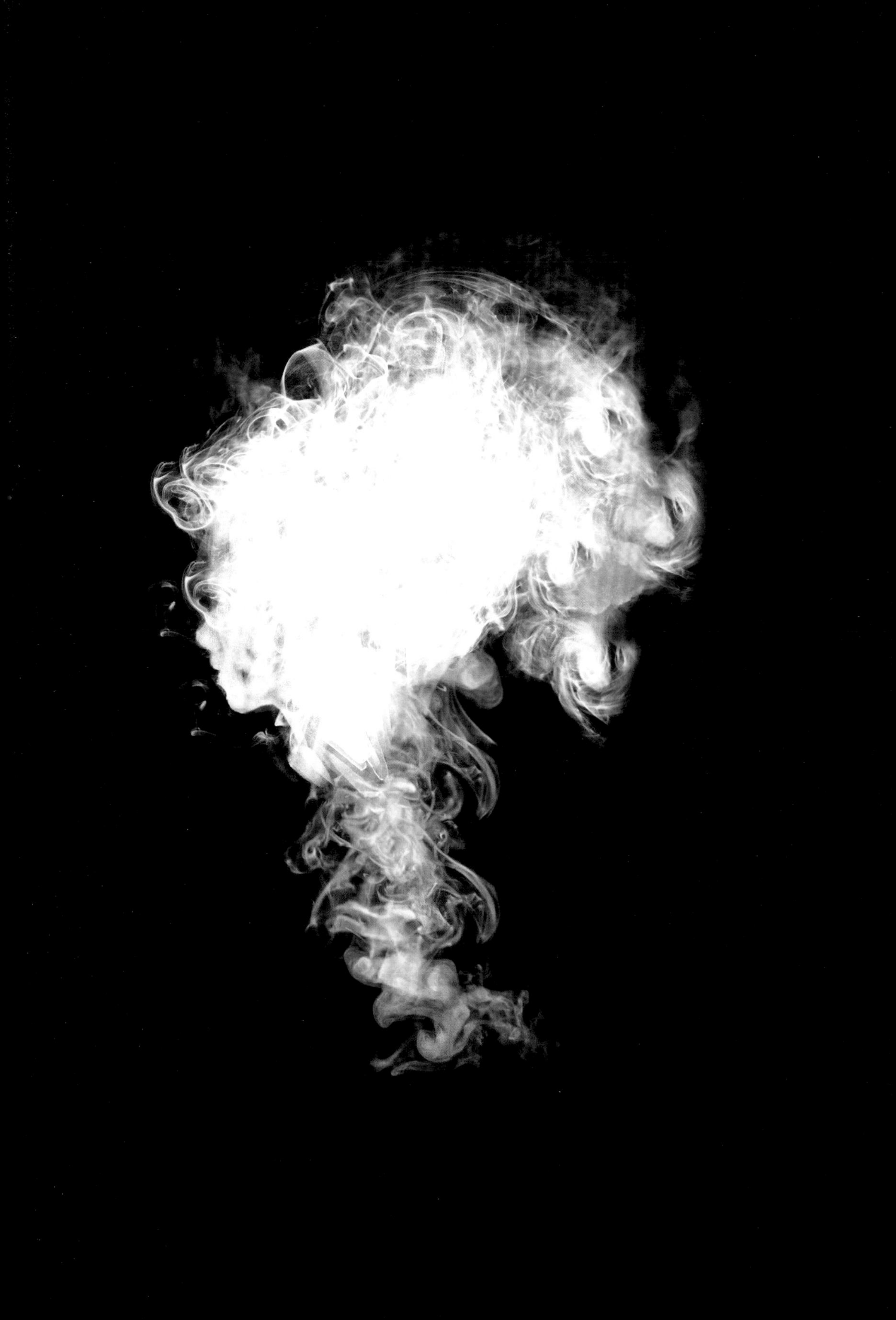

VERA'S LIST . WRITTEN BY TYRONE FINCH. ART BY TODD HARRIS

IGBO LANDING . WRITTEN BY MELODY COOPER. ART BY EDER MESSIAS

OUSLEY . WRITTEN BY GREG BURNHAM. ART BY MARCUS WILLIAMS

ENTANGLEMENT . WRITTEN BY ERIKA HARDISON. ART BY KAREN S.DARBOE

HART OF THE MATTER . WRITTEN BY DAVID WALKER. ART BY MARK BRIGHT

GEMINI VISIONS . WRITTEN BY BRANDON EASTON. ART BY DIETRICH SMITH

AFTERWORD

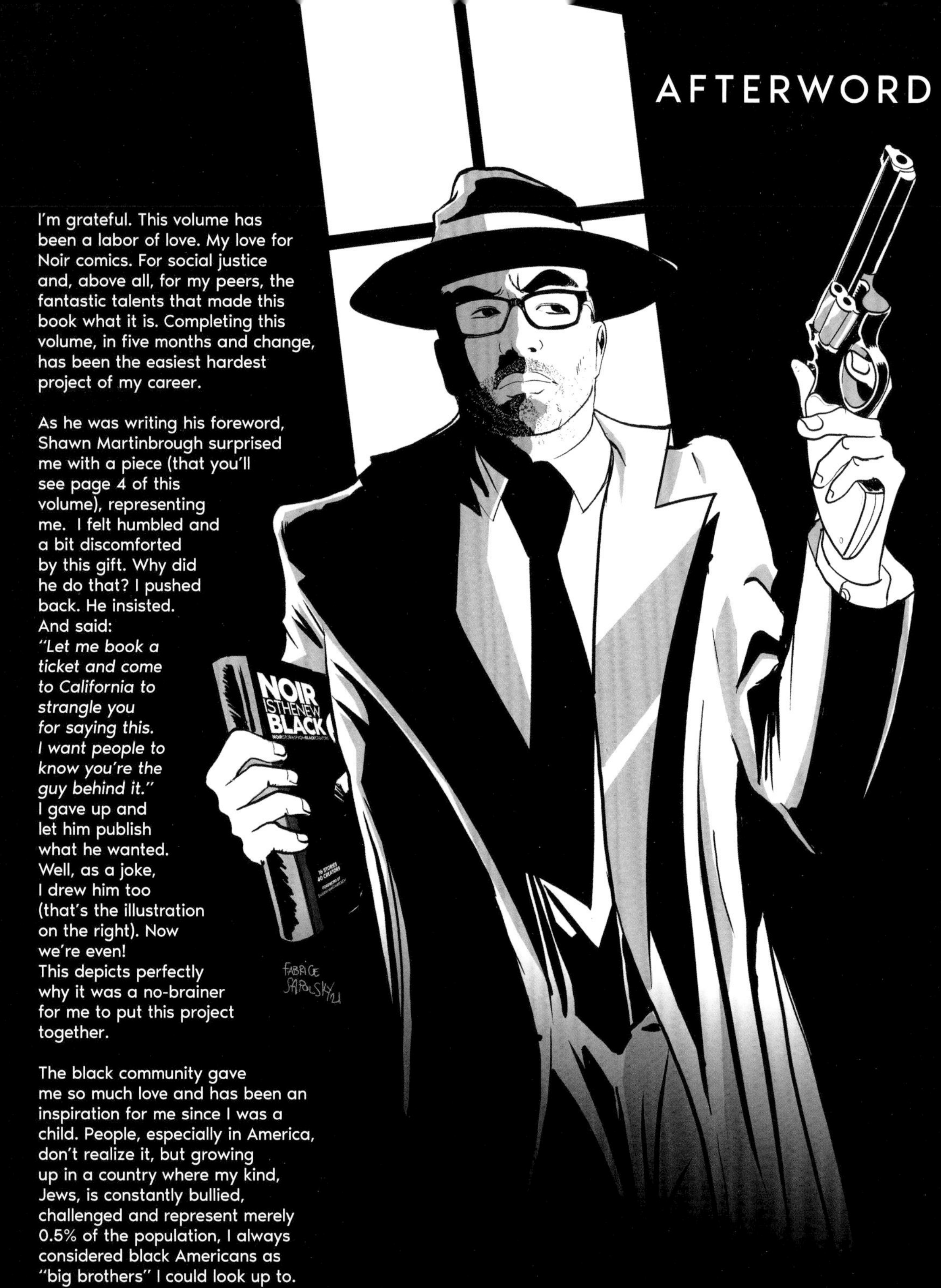

I'm grateful. This volume has been a labor of love. My love for Noir comics. For social justice and, above all, for my peers, the fantastic talents that made this book what it is. Completing this volume, in five months and change, has been the easiest hardest project of my career.

As he was writing his foreword, Shawn Martinbrough surprised me with a piece (that you'll see page 4 of this volume), representing me. I felt humbled and a bit discomforted by this gift. Why did he do that? I pushed back. He insisted. And said: *"Let me book a ticket and come to California to strangle you for saying this. I want people to know you're the guy behind it."* I gave up and let him publish what he wanted. Well, as a joke, I drew him too (that's the illustration on the right). Now we're even! This depicts perfectly why it was a no-brainer for me to put this project together.

The black community gave me so much love and has been an inspiration for me since I was a child. People, especially in America, don't realize it, but growing up in a country where my kind, Jews, is constantly bullied, challenged and represent merely 0.5% of the population, I always considered black Americans as "big brothers" I could look up to.

We lived parallel lives. Our collective and individual pains have been different through History. But our ability to transcend our condition through creativity and art is similar. I am an ally and a friend, an immigrant and a minority.

With *Noir is the New Black*, I wanted to give back some of that love and take a stand. FairSquare Comics will always be a home for minorities and immigrant creators.

We'll keep creating comics for the rest of us. It's our *raison d'être*. Again, I want to thank creators and the 1167 Kickstarter backers who helped bringing this project to life.
And a special dedication to my friend and co-editor, TC Harris: It's been a roller coaster but I guess we changed each other's life. Without TC, this collection wouldn't exist either.
80 years ago, minorities (jewish and italian immigrants) created the comic book industry. Let's never forget where we come from and let's move forward together. That goes without saying, this is not the last Black Noir book you'll read from FairSquare Comics.

To be continued...

Fabrice Sapolsky,
Publisher